The Mirror of the Soul

J. Lloyd Morgan

Based on the songs of Chris de Burgh

ISBN-10: 0988633027
ISBN-13: 978-0988633025

Edited by: Tristi Pinkston

To Chris: whose songs have touched the lives of so many.

INTRODUCTION

When I first heard the song for which this book is named, I thought, "Wow. That would make a wonderful book." Most sane people would have let the idea stop there. But each time I listened to the song, the more I was convinced that I should at least try. To my surprise, and delight, I was able to get not only permission, but encouragement to write this book from Chris de Burgh and his management.

In order to flush out a single song into a novel, I elected to interweave several of Chris de Burgh's songs into the main story. (Again, with permission.) In addition, there are dozens upon dozens of references to yet even more songs.

And in the end, I am pleased to present a book that I believe stands on its own, but also pays respect to the idea and philosophy behind the song.

AMOR SPECULUM ANIMA LUCET.

LUCIFER EX INFERNO CLAMAT.

NE NOS INDUCAT IN TENTATIONEM.

AMOR SPECULUM ANIMA LUCET.

Prologue

Dordogne region of France, the year of our Lord 1453

Somewhere … a lonely man tries sleeping …

Geoffrey had tried to go to sleep. He honestly had. At least that's what he kept telling himself. Yes, most certainly, sleep had been given a fair chance. But the stillness of the night was too much to bear. The scant noises here and there weren't consistent or powerful enough to distract his mind.

It had been a full rotation of seasons since his sweet wife, Zoe, had passed on. An autumn, winter, spring and summer had come and gone, yet the pain of her death still seemed as fresh as the day she died.

At her funeral, he recited some words he had learned to say on such occasions. They spoke of life being temporary, and how every person must cherish each moment. The words gave him very little comfort on nights like these—nights when he couldn't sleep.

He let out a frustrated sigh and sat up, throwing the covers to the side. His actions caught the attention of Roquet, his dog, who had been asleep by the fireplace. The mutt's head perked up and looked directly at Geoffrey, his tail starting to wag ever so slightly.

Geoffrey swung his legs over the side of the bed. "Say we go for a walk, eh, old friend?" Roquet responded by wagging his tail more enthusiastically.

The night was dark, with an autumn nip in the air. Most of the leaves had fallen from the trees around his modest house—a house which stood, fairly isolated, on a hill north of the town that surrounded the Abbé St. Pierre.

Geoffrey exhaled, and even though he had only the light of the stars to see by, his breath was visible in front of him. Though he was wearing his heaviest cloak, he felt the chill start to seep into his bones. He reconsidered for a moment, thinking about his warm bed. But then he would be back to his thoughts—thoughts of loved ones long gone. No, he had promised Roquet a walk, and a walk Roquet would get.

"Of course you'd have to pick a night with a new moon to go for a walk, wouldn't you, Roquet?" Geoffrey asked. The dog just kept wagging his tail, with his long, pink tongue hanging from one side of his mouth.

Geoffrey pulled his cloak around him tighter and started walking. He didn't have a particular destination—just somewhere to fill his mind with other thoughts.

The crunching of leaves was all he heard, aside from the occasional sound of a nocturnal animal. Roquet would always cower when he heard a sound he didn't like. He had been that way ever since…

No. Geoffrey didn't want to think about that. It was hard enough keeping thoughts of his dead wife from his mind, and he doubted he'd ever sleep again if he started to dwell on the demise of his two sons.

Ahead, an animal of some sort scurried off into the bushes. Roquet's brave reaction was to tuck his tail between his legs and hide behind Geoffrey.

"Not much of a watchdog, are you, boy?" Geoffrey asked. He reached down and scratched the mutt behind his ears. Roquet looked up at Geoffrey and smiled the way only dogs could. Geoffrey smiled back, but then noticed that Roquet was no longer looking at him, but *beyond* him, up toward the sky.

Geoffrey followed his dog's gaze and saw what had caught his attention. A star in the sky seemed to be glowing brighter than the ones around it. *That's odd*, Geoffrey thought. He had lived here all his life and had spent many a night staring at the sky. He knew the star patterns by heart, and he didn't recall a bright star in that part of the sky.

Perhaps it was his imagination, but Geoffrey thought that the star was actually becoming brighter. How was that possible? For a moment longer he watched. Then he was sure; the star was becoming brighter, and it seemed to be getting longer. *Longer? How could a star grow longer?*

With a start, Geoffrey realized that the star itself wasn't getting longer or brighter—it was coming toward him. A blazing trail of fire in the wake of the falling object had given the illusion of it lengthening out.

Part of Geoffrey's mind shouted for him to run, but his body froze and another part of his mind watched the falling object in wonder. Sound now accompanied the sight, a low rumbling, like thunder, only growing louder as the star approached.

Before he could will his body to react, the

object flew overhead, crashing into the forest just beyond.

A peculiar light lingered after the object hit the ground, and then dimmed to a feeble glow. With the impact, Geoffrey's senses returned to him. Certainly this was something beyond his comprehension. He turned to run, until he noticed that Roquet had started to trot toward the light.

"Roquet!" Geoffrey cried out, but the dog kept making for the trees. Something was certainly amiss. Roquet was afraid of *everything.* Why would he approach the object that had fallen from the sky so readily?

Geoffrey screwed up his courage and followed. By the time he caught up, Roquet had gone through the trees and had made his way down into a crater formed by the object's impact, probably half a man's height deep.

Again, Geoffrey called out, "Roquet! Get back here, you mangy mutt! You don't know what that is!"

Roquet's reaction was to sniff the object that Geoffrey couldn't quite make out. His normally anxious companion was showing no signs of fear. That, in and of itself, was a miracle.

Several more times Geoffrey tried to get Roquet to come out of the crater, but to no avail. Cursing under his breath, Geoffrey began to climb down. The object was still emitting a weak light and the closer Geoffrey got to it, the more in focus it became. *This couldn't be!* It was a diamond, as big as his two hands. Roquet was still sniffing the diamond, and Geoffrey noticed that the dog's tail was wagging.

Unable to curb his curiosity, Geoffrey held his palm out toward the diamond. He had seen a trail of fire following the object as it fell; surely it would be burning to the touch. Yet he could feel no heat coming from it. He shouldn't touch it. He should just leave it be.

He was a simple man, not one to make such discoveries. At the same time, he couldn't leave it here. If word got out that a large diamond had been found in these woods, it soon would be crawling with treasure hunters—or worse. Geoffrey had seen firsthand what greedy men were capable of doing. After all, the long war between France and England had finally come to an end, but not before his two sons had paid the price with their blood. He realized he had thought about his two sons, despite the promise to himself that he wouldn't. *Why am I reminded about them tonight?*

The diamond couldn't remain here to be found by someone who would use it for evil purposes. Such things could start wars. He wouldn't permit another war to start if he could help it. He loved his sons too much to allow more parents to experience the pain he felt.

Geoffrey set his feet and went to lift the diamond. *For you, my sons.* When he placed his hands on the sides of the object, a light almost as bright as the sun erupted from the diamond.

Chapter 1

"We must send the devil to the fire!" Abbot Ignace shouted at his monks from the pulpit.

The four of them responded with looks that Ignace interpreted as stunned surprise. They sat on the front pews of the chapel, as they did every day at this time. "I've heard your grumblings, not only from your mouths when you thought I wasn't listening, but also from your stomachs. The townspeople are no longer bringing in the donations to which we are accustomed. Who can tell me why?"

Brother Sabastien, or Bastien as he was commonly called, spoke first. "Certainly it has to do with the end of the war. People are no longer as afraid. They've become complacent—they're beginning to forget the Lord."

"Forget the Lord, you say?" Ignace asked incredulously. "Forget the Lord because there is no war? Are you telling me that the evils of war bring men closer to the Lord?"

The diminutive stature of Brother Bastien appeared to shrink further at the abbot's questions.

Ignace looked to the other monks. "Well? What say you?"

Brother Jehan, the polar opposite of Brother Bastien in size, merely shrugged his huge shoulders in response.

Brother Florent, who was lean but quick, looked as if he was about to say something, but then appeared to change his mind.

Finally, Brother Maximilien broke the silence. He did not meet the abbot's glare, instead he wrapped the end of his long, snowy beard around one of his fingers as he spoke. "Perhaps it's because we are to blame, Abbot. Perhaps we're not worthy of such donations."

Ignace tightly gripped the sides of the pulpit in front of him, causing his fingers to change color from the pressure. The monks began to shift noticeably on their cushioned benches. "Yes! Exactly! Brother Maximilien is correct. It's because of the sins of the monks in this, the Abbé St. Pierre, that we're being punished. You've become slothful. You only bring me townspeople who want to discuss their petty concerns and irritating problems instead of properly inspiring them to bring donations."

He stopped and looked at each of the monks in turn. "You have all let the devil into your hearts. He has his eye fixed firmly on each of you. You can't escape him, not without the Lord's help. Not without *my* help. Each of you must pray for guidance. Pray for forgiveness. Pray for an answer to have your sins washed from you. Then, and only then, will the townspeople return to donating to the Abbé as they should. We're far too important to be suffering on the meager supplies we now collect."

He stood, his short and rotund figure not rising much higher than when he was sitting. "Go! Go now and repent!"

ଔଓ

Ambre was simply the most beautiful creature the Lord had ever made; at least, that was Brother Jehan's opinion. Her hair was raven black and framed her slender face perfectly. Her deep blue eyes were only outdone by her red, full lips—lips that always curved into a smile when she saw Brother Jehan approaching.

"Good day to you, Brother Jehan," Ambre said in her soft, smooth way of speaking.

The large monk felt his heart beating faster as he approached her. "And good day to you as well, Mademoiselle."

Her right eyebrow arched slightly at the comment. "Mademoiselle now, is it? Why so formal?"

"You never know who may be watching…or listening," Jehan said. He looked around carefully.

Ambre stepped out from behind the table that held her wares. She sold produce for several of the farmers in the area, and though there were others who sold equally good vegetables and fruits, Ambre was able to fetch a higher price and had a more loyal client base, no doubt due to her flirtatious nature and attractive features. Her table was set up next to several others in the merchant district. The heavy traffic packed down the dirt in the area, keeping it from becoming too muddy during rainstorms.

"Afraid someone may overhear you buying potatoes, is that it?" She placed one finger on his chest and slowly moved it downward.

Jehan reached up quickly and took her hand, startling Ambre.

"Please," he whispered fiercely, "don't do that. Not where someone could report it to the abbot."

"Ah, I understand." Ambre smiled and removed her hand from his. "You're afraid that the abbot will banish you from the Abbé now, eh? And so what if he does? The war is over. Both you and I know why you became a monk. You should leave the Monastery. There is much out here to enjoy. And you are much too handsome to be a monk."

He knew that women found him attractive; before he became a monk, he had never lacked for the company of a pretty woman. It was one of many things he had given up when he joined the Monastery.

She looked up at him with those eyes that made his stomach do flips. "All you have to do is say yes and I'll be with you," she cooed.

For a moment Jehan considered the offer. It was true that he became a monk to escape conscription into one of the armies. While he had to suffer through long sermons and wasn't able to get as drunk as he would like, or pursue women, he was well treated. At least, he had been until recently. During the war, he always had his fill to eat. His room was warm and dry and he slept in a comfortable bed. The donations from the townspeople were generous, mainly because the abbot promised protection to those who would give freely to the Abbé. But all that was starting to change. What if he were to leave? He could have Ambre, something he highly desired. But, then, what would he do to make money? Work at the Abbé was easy enough.

Aside from the tasks assigned to him by Abbot

Ignace, he would also take turns listening to the confessions of the townspeople, something he found to be quite entertaining. No. While his desire for Ambre was strong, he couldn't risk giving up the easy life.

"I'm sorry," he said. "I can't."

Ambre stared at him a moment and then folded her arms over her chest. "More likely, you mean, that you won't. There's a difference." She sighed. "A shame. I'd show you what it means to be a man."

Jehan felt the pull of temptation now stronger than ever. Who would have to know? But the risk of the abbot finding out was too high. If Jehan wasn't brave enough to go to war, he certainly wasn't brave enough to risk the wrath of Abbot Ignace.

"I must leave," he said, and turned to do so.

"But you didn't buy anything yet," she pointed out.

He frowned a bit at the truth. If he returned without the food, that would also upset the abbot. He grunted in acceptance of her statement and made his purchase. After paying Ambre, he said, "Until next time."

Ambre's response was to say, "My offer remains, Jehan. It will always remain."

೧೫೨

Brother Jehan sat on a padded chair next to the Abbé's only gate as he did every evening. The abbot considered the time just after the sun set as the most dangerous.

Though the war was over, Ignace feared that

marauding bands of brigands and robbers would be about. As the largest of the monks, Jehan did an excellent job keeping the unwanted people out of the Abbé.

He sat under a steep overhang that kept the elements off him, which was especially welcomed this evening, the night of the first snow. He didn't know much about such things, but from what he understood, it looked like it would be a heavy snow tonight. But before too long, he would be in his warm room on his comfortable bed. It was a reaffirmation that he had made the right choice to stay at the Abbé.

A knock on the gate startled him. Certainly the townspeople had learned not to bother the monks so late in the day. He himself had made it very clear that unless you had something substantial to offer, you weren't welcomed. And he was comfortable on his chair, all wrapped up in a thick quilt. Perhaps if he ignored the person, they would go away.

The knock sounded again, and then a third time. Mumbling a curse under his breath, Brother Jehan stood up and opened the shutter to the gate's small hatch.

He was taken aback by what he saw. On the other side of the gate was a girl. Her hair was as golden as the sun on the warmest summer day. She wore a cloak of varying shades of green, but it was her eyes that were the most remarkable. There was something so alive, so fresh about them.

"Please, kind sir, I am seeking food and bed for the night." Her voice sounded like a warm spring breeze.

She seemed so innocent, so full of life. But

Brother Jehan was under strict orders. "What do you have to offer?"

The girl simply shrugged. "I'm not sure what you mean."

"None are allowed to stay at the Abbé unless they have a substantial donation to make—it's well known around here."

She drew her cloak tighter around her. "I'm a traveler. I'm not aware of such things. Please, sir, it's cold and I've no place to stay."

Brother Jehan looked deep into her eyes—eyes that held something familiar. It was something he couldn't place. Though part of him wanted to help her, he knew that even giving her coin from his own pocket would make the abbot upset if he was caught.

"There's no shelter for you here. Move along."

She looked at him once again, this time with unmistakable sadness on her face. He closed the hatch so he wouldn't have to look at her. He stood there for a moment, staring at the shutter. It had been painted this past summer with a new color that was very expensive, but amazingly attractive. The painter called the color "satin green," which reminded him of spring. With a start, Jehan realized that the girl's eyes had the same effect. They reminded him of a time he wouldn't see for several months—his favorite time of the year, April.

ঔঌ

"Look! It's starting to snow!" Lucien said excitedly.

Christophe looked up to the grey-covered sky

and could make out the winter's first flakes falling slowly toward the earth. "That it is, my boy. That it is, which means we better hurry home before we get covered. You know your mother will give us a scolding if she thinks we've been playing in the snow when she has supper ready."

"May I at least stay out long enough to catch a snowflake on my tongue? It's supposed to be good luck."

Christophe admired his twelve-year-old's childlike wonder, even if he should have grown out of it by now. He also enjoyed that his son came every evening to meet him at the shop to walk home with him after the work was done for the day. The walk through the streets of the town that surrounded the Abbé St. Pierre wasn't far, and it gave them a chance to talk before he got home. "Not tonight, Lucien. We must hurry home. Remember, it's my night at the tavern."

The boy looked crestfallen. His dark hair, much like Christophe's, had started to accumulate white flakes of snow. "I forgot. I guess the snow distracted me." Lucien looked up at his father. "You know that mother worries about you when you're at the tavern, don't you, Father?"

Christophe was startled. "She has told you this?"

"Not as such, no," Lucien admitted. "But I can tell. After she thinks I've gone to bed, she waits by the window, looking out into the night for you."

This revelation bothered Christophe. His wife, Rosette, was the inspiration for many of the tales he told and songs he sung. She had always been supportive of his entertaining at one of the local taverns, knowing how much he enjoyed it. It was certainly more fulfilling than his days of selling various items for Didier, a wealthy merchant who brought in items from faraway places. He wished he could make a living from singing songs and spinning stories, and probably could do so if it was just himself he needed to support. Once he had married the love of his life and they'd had Lucien, he'd decided to take more steady work to make sure they were kept warm with full bellies.

"I'll keep it short tonight," Christophe said lightly, trying to brighten the mood. "If it continues to snow like this, I'm sure the tavern patrons will head home before it gets too deep."

ଔଓ

Christophe held the audience's full attention. He told a story of lovers in the war who stayed together 'til the rain had to fall. It was one of Christophe's favorite tales, filled with wonderful phrases and words. Even the tavern's owner, Jourdain, stood and watched, his hands still, though he was holding a rag and a mug he had been cleaning.

The tavern wasn't the largest in the area, but it was the cleanest. It had a decent sized common area with a high ceiling. There was a second story where people could rent rooms, and from the talk of the patrons, the beds were comfortable and bug free.

It was moments like these that Christophe looked forward to the most. He had been told many a time that he had a gift—and a gift like his needed to be shared. The look in the eyes of his audience was worth more to him than any amount of gold. Unfortunately, it was gold that seemed to rule the world. Well, gold and greed. Perhaps Christophe would write a story one day about the foolishness of such slippery pursuits.

The tavern patrons clapped appreciatively as Christophe finished.

"More! More!" they cried.

Coins were tossed into a glass jar on a nearby table to encourage him to continue.

"Alas, my friends," Christophe said, "I've made a promise to my family to be home earlier tonight."

There were a few shouts of disapproval, as well as a glare from the owner of the tavern.

"I promise to return next week with another story, or two or three…"

"Or four!" shouted someone at the back of the crowd.

Christophe smiled and the crowd chuckled at the comment.

"Or four," Christophe agreed, and then left the modest stage.

He worked his way through the crowd, shaking hands and thanking them for coming. He finally arrived at his destination, in front of the tavern's owner. The man was older, with more hair growing out of his ears than on the top of his head. Jourdain had collected the jar and was counting out the coins.

"Thirty-three tonight. Not a bad haul on the first snowy evening," Jourdain said.

He then counted out three of the coins and handed them to Christophe. "Here's your share. Next week, I want you to stay longer, get me? We could have maybe doubled this once they got a few more drinks in them."

"I'll be here next week," Christophe promised, then turned and walked out into the snowy night.

ଔ

The knock on the wooden gate was faint. It was so faint, in fact, that it was hardly a knock at all. It was more like a soft tapping, as if the person was afraid to disturb anyone inside, or perhaps they lacked the strength to knock more forcefully.

"Did you hear that, boy?" Geoffrey asked Roquet. His dog responded by cowering under the table.

Geoffrey sighed. "I guess that means you did hear something. It's probably just another one of those strangers asking me if I saw what fell from the sky, or if I knew what made that hole in the ground nearby."

He glanced over to the cupboard where he had hidden the diamond. "Maybe we should rid ourselves of it, eh Roquet? If anyone finds it, they may kill us for it. Yet, the way it shines and the way I feel when I touch it… There is something special about this diamond."

There was more knocking, this time even fainter. "All right, stay here, you mutt. I'll see who it is and shoo them away. It may be tough.

"If they are foolish enough to be out on a snowy night like this, they may not leave easily. You may have to actually act like a guard dog and bark at them."

Roquet laid his head on the floor and tucked in his tail behind him. Grunting as he stood, Geoffrey wished he had brought in more firewood. Though he had a fire going, his wood supply wouldn't last more than a couple of days, and he didn't enjoy the thought of digging more firewood out from under the snow. This house was one of the few that had a proper fireplace built inside. It was once a hunting lodge for a rich merchant, Geoffrey's former employer. When the merchant was killed in the war many years ago, Geoffrey brought his family here, and no one seemed to question it. With battles raging around them, people had more important things to worry about.

Geoffrey donned his cloak and creaked open his front door. The gate at the end of the front path was a good twenty paces away—just far enough that he could see a shape, but he was unable to make out who was there in the darkness of the snowy night.

"Go away!" he shouted. "I've not seen what you are looking for! Now go away before I have my battle hound attack you!"

There was a soft whimper from Roquet after this statement.

"Please, sir," a soft female voice said. "Please, I only…"

Geoffrey watched as she fell to the ground. Putting all other thoughts aside, he threw the door open and rushed out to the gate.

On the ground was a girl in a green dress. She looked so fragile. Certainly she wasn't here to steal the diamond.

He opened the gate and scooped the girl out of the ankle-deep snow. Her eyes were closed and her skin was almost as white as the snow that fell around him. Without bothering to close the gate, he rushed her inside, shut the door, and set her down by the fire.

She was breathing, but only just. Geoffrey tore the blankets off his bed and covered her as best he could. *What is she doing out here? Where's her family?* he thought.

Geoffrey stood and went to gather the items needed to make some tea. Surely the girl must be nearly frozen. He opened his cupboards and frantically searched for his teapot.

He heard the sound of Roquet panting happily behind him. He turned, hands still in the cupboard, and saw his dog curled up next to the girl.

She had slid one of her hands out from under the blankets and was petting Roquet.

When she looked at Geoffrey, her eyes were like none he had seen before. They held a certain light and hope in them, though the light seemed to be fading.

Geoffrey began to say something, but as he went to move from the cupboard, he bumped the covered diamond, causing it to glow brightly, even though it was wrapped in cloth.

The girl's eyes grew wide. She tried to say something, but only a whisper escaped her lips. Geoffrey went to her side. "What's that, my dear?"

She pointed to the wrapped diamond. "Will you bring it here?" she said in a voice that sounded like a spring zephyr.

Geoffrey had been scared to let anyone know of the diamond's existence, yet his heart told him that this innocent girl meant him no harm. He nodded and stood. Carefully he removed the diamond, and it glowed again as soon as he touched it, lighting up the room. He brought it next to her and unwrapped it so she could see it in all its glory.

"Speculum anima," she said reverently.

Geoffrey shook his head. "I don't understand."

She looked at him and smiled. "It means, 'the mirror of the soul.'"

Gently she reached out and touched the diamond. Instead of the bright white light that was emitted when Geoffrey touched it, the light was now various shades of gold and green. It reminded him of his youth, when life was new and full of promise. It was the first time in recent memory when the ache in his heart for his fallen loved ones was replaced by joy.

"Thank you," he said, crying openly.

She removed her hand from the diamond and smiled at him—a smile that stayed with her even after the life and light in her eyes dimmed out.

The next day Geoffrey buried the girl gently and good in his family's plot. It wasn't easy to do so. He had to clear the earth of snow first, and then dig into the cold ground. Yet he felt he could do nothing less for her. She was a girl he didn't know and couldn't save, and yet she had shared something remarkable with him.

He looked to the sky. "It appears we have more snow on the way, Roquet. But it doesn't matter. Tomorrow we head out for the Abbé. Certainly the clever monks will know what to do with the diamond—or as she called it, the mirror of the soul."

Chapter 2

Geoffrey woke later than he had expected. He wanted to get an early start, but digging the grave the previous day had been quite taxing on his aged body, making it difficult for him to get out of bed. "C'mon, Roquet," he said as he rose. "Even if we leave soon, we won't arrive until nightfall."

Carefully, Geoffrey placed the diamond in a large, leather bag which he usually used to gather tubers and other vegetables from his garden. While the diamond would shine if he touched it through cloth, leather appeared to be thick enough to keep it from glowing. After putting on his cloak, he said, "I guess we should pay our respects before we go, eh, old friend?" Roquet's answer was to wag his tail furiously.

The sun had risen and was shining brightly in the sky; the world was snow-white. It appeared that a good amount of snow had fallen during the evening. Even with the sun up, the air was brisk. Geoffrey felt the cold already bleeding through his cloak. His family's cemetery plot was just down the hill, beyond a small grove.

It took effort to trudge through the deep snow, but Geoffrey was convinced he needed guidance when it came to this diamond. Things were happening that he didn't understand. If he had not seen them for himself, he would certainly doubt anyone telling him such stories. A diamond that fell from the sky? An object that shone when touched? A young girl who showed up at his gate in a snowstorm and, in her dying moments, touched the diamond and filled him with joy? Certainly any one of these stories would be enough to have him locked up for being wrong in the head. He needed to seek out the monks now, before anything else strange happened. However, Geoffrey didn't get his wish. Upon rounding the bend in the grove that led to the cemetery, his eyes once again beheld something that shouldn't be.

The field was ablaze with flowers on the grave of the girl he had buried the night before.

Christophe's mind wandered as he made the familiar trek to his place of employment. The street lined with modest houses was quiet this early in the morning. His boss, Didier, had been in an overall dour mood since the war ended. There was profit to be made in war, especially for a merchant who imported and exported items. During the war, carts that normally carried various household items also hid weapons in secret compartments. These weapons would be sold for a hefty profit, which in turn made Didier a wealthy man.

Now, such items were much less in demand, and people were just starting to buy luxury items that just a few short years ago had been impossible to find.

However, they were bought in small quantities and only occasionally, whereas the weapons always sold out quickly and for a higher profit.

It once again brought to his mind how the pursuit of worldly power and wealth were everywhere, and yet, even if someone had plenty, they always wanted more.

The work Christophe performed for Didier was simple enough: he was the face of the store. Didier was not a handsome man. He wore a thick beard and mustache to hide the scars earned from a sickness he'd had as a child. In addition, his eyes seemed too small and close together in relation to his thick nose. Include that his earlobes drooped almost as low as his chin and it was no wonder that the general public wanted nothing to do with him. While Didier knew how to talk to merchants and was a master in the art of bargaining, he was not as successful in relating to the common townsperson. That's where Christophe came in. He was well liked, not only for his quick smile and wit, but also because he was sincere in his dealings with his fellow man. His philosophy was "sell them the right item for their needs, and they will return, making more money for the store in the long run." So far, it had served him well.

Didier was already at La boutique de désirs, his store, as indicated by smoke coming from the chimney. Christophe had always thought the name to be a bit pretentious, but any store that offered to sell what people desired definitely got attention. He knocked on the door a few times, then rubbed his hands together. Snow had fallen again last night, bringing the total up to his mid-calf.

"Christophe," Didier said in greeting after he opened the door. "You're late."

It was the same routine every morning. No

matter what time Christophe arrived, Didier always claimed he was late. Christophe figured it was the other man's way of putting him on the defensive while at the same time allowing Didier to make it clear who was in charge.

"As you say, Didier," Christophe said, not making eye contact.

Christophe removed his cloak and hung it on a brass peg by the front door. The store was fairly large, with a dozen or so rows of merchandise. There was a storage area in the loft above the main floor, as well as some that could be placed in Didier's office in the back. Christophe knew where everything was by heart as he not only sold the items, but stocked them as well.

"Are we still expecting the shipment from Bordeaux today?" Christophe asked. "I'd imagine that with the snow, they might be delayed."

Didier frowned. "They'd better not be late. I'm paying a fortune for that load."

The owner then turned to Christophe. "I'm off to go hunting. Keep the store open until the sun sets. I've made an inventory, so I'll know if you take anything while I'm gone."

Again, it was the same threat every time Didier went hunting, which was often. The man didn't need the meat or skins; he enjoyed killing.

"The only things that will be gone are what I sell," Christophe assured him. "If the shipment does make it in today, I'll have the driver sign the shipping list with me, all right?"

Didier didn't seem to hear him. He was gathering his hunting gear and putting on his heavy winter coat.

"Just make sure that if the shipment arrives, you have the driver sign the list as well as you, got it?" Didier commanded.

Christophe fought off a sigh. "Excellent suggestion, boss. Good luck on your hunt."

"Luck?" Didier laughed. "I don't need luck."

With that, the unpleasant man left the store.

ᏳᏰᏊ

Abbot Ignace grinned at his reflection. His naturally curly hair bounced when he shook his head. His smile was stunning, with a proper gap between his front teeth. That was a sign of a truly blessed person, and he liked how it caused his words to whistle slightly when he spoke. It gave him an air of dignity—he spoke like no one around him.

It was going to be another glorious day. It promised to be a bit cool, which would allow him to wear his favorite fur-lined cape. The fact that it was fox fur made it even more splendid. He looked marvelous in red.

Sadly, however, fewer people were attending church and giving donations. *It's a shame not to be seen in such a wonderful cape.*

Brother Maximilien had been by earlier. The monk was fat and ugly. There were no better words to describe him. Ignace held up a dainty hand to his mouth as he giggled at the thought of Maximilien ever looking as wonderful as this.

The monk's parents must have been terrible sinners for them to give birth to such a thickly built boy.

Maximilien did have his uses. He was good

with numbers and had been assigned to the treasury. Ignace didn't worry about the monk stealing from him. As long as Maximilien had his fill to eat, he was loyal.

That hadn't been a problem until recently. Maximilien's latest report indicated that the treasury was at an all-time low, even with the cutbacks on spending they had made. This wouldn't do. No, this wouldn't do at all.

Perhaps Ignace should think of a way to remedy this problem. But he had lectured the monks that it was their fault, and he believed it. They were the problem here, not him.

Take Brother Bastien as an example. The mousy man was in charge of preparing the meals, yet the sun was up and he had yet to deliver breakfast. Ignace would have to give a lecture to Bastien about making better use of his time. Well, he needed to do something while he waited. Perhaps he could start to work on his next sermon. Bah, why bother? *I have plenty I've written before. I'll just use one of those.* The people were blessed just to hear him speak; it didn't really matter what he said. Perhaps, instead, he would just sit here and admire himself some more in the mirror. Yes, that was a superb idea.

ଓଃ

"The abbot's bound to be in a foul mood," Brother Maximilien said. "Another day's passed with no donations. Our food supplies are running low. I've heard him say that he may have to make one of the monks go to a different Abbé if things don't improve soon."

This was exactly what Brother Jehan had feared might happen. As the youngest of the monks, it would most likely be him sent away. "I don't know what else to do," Jehan said. "I've told anyone who comes to the gate that they need to prove their worthiness by donating more if they want to see the abbot, but most just get angry and walk away. Are you telling me that no one stopped by today?"

Brother Maximilien had been watching the gate for most of the afternoon, and Brother Jehan had come to take over.

"Not a soul. Perhaps you'll be more blessed."

Maximilien went to stand, but then stopped. "Would you like me to take your shift?"

"Why would you offer to do that?" Jehan asked, suspicion seeping into his voice. "It's cold and snowy out here. Aren't you looking forward to a warm meal?"

The fat monk looked at Jehan, wringing his hands as he spoke. "I don't mind. We are all doing the Lord's work. Allow me this charity."

Jehan knew better. Maximilien loved to eat. However, with the abbot upset, no one wanted to be around him—even to the point of missing a meal and staying out in the cold. Jehan had quickly eaten his meal before the abbot had officially arrived and came to take over the gate duty early for the same reason.

"But how can I show the Lord I am worthy if I let you do my tasks? Thank you for the offer, but I insist," Jehan replied, trying to sound sincere.

He knew that Maximilien couldn't force the issue, even though he was his senior. The portly monk sighed and then stood up.

"All right, Brother," he said. "I shall make sure that Brother Florent remembers to relieve you at the proper time."

Jehan pulled the heavy brown cowl over his head to cover his face and settled into the chair. In no time, he had dozed off, his dreams filled with visions of Ambre. It was summer, and she was in the fields, by the river. She wore a simple dress that left little to the imagination. Her long hair cascaded over her bare shoulders. She noticed him and beckoned for him to come to her.

Once again, he felt the pull of temptation. He stood in place, struggling with what to do. At that moment, there was a loud banging at the wooden gate that was set into the high, limestone walls of the Abbé.

Jehan woke up startled, stood, then opened the small shutter in the door and peered out. "What do you want?" the monk demanded gruffly.

On the other side of the gate was an older man. He had a bag of some sort slung over one shoulder. Next to him was the ugliest dog Jehan had ever seen.

"Good Brother, my name is Geoffrey," the man said as an introduction. "I have something I would like you to see." He motioned to the bag he was carrying.

"What is it, then?" Jehan asked.

Geoffrey swung the bag from over his shoulder and into his hands. "It's something that came from the sky. Certainly it must be from another world."

There had been talk of a light in the sky recently and rumors of something landing nearby, but no one claimed to have found it—until now. Jehan heard someone approaching from behind him.

He turned to see that it was Brother Florent, a monk, like himself, who had joined the Monastery to avoid fighting in the war.

Jehan called out to Florent, "Brother, there's a man at the gate, he has something in his hand; he says it fell down from the sky, should I let him in?"

Florent walked to Jehan and pulled him away from the gate. In a subdued voice, he said, "Maybe it's an omen, maybe it will take away our sin."

Brother Jehan was confused at first. He didn't believe the reason the donations had stopped was because he had been sinning. Florent appeared to pick up on that and said again, "Our sin …" Then he motioned his head toward the abbot's residence. "Discover what it is."

Peeking his head back out the hatch, Jehan asked, "What did you find?"

Geoffrey responded by removing the object from the bag. As soon as his hand touched it, an almost blinding light shone from the object.

"Cover it up! Quickly!" Jehan instructed.

The old man did as he was told.

"What is it?" Jehan whispered.

"I was told it was called 'the mirror of the soul'. I'm not sure why, though," Geoffrey responded.

None of this made any sense. What object would shine like that? And why would the old man know what to call it, but not why? He turned again to Florent. "'Tis a diamond that he has, the biggest one I've ever seen. And when he holds it in his hand, it's shining like the sun. He says it's from another world—he calls it the mirror of the soul."

Florent got a strange look in his eye, something Jehan hadn't seen before.

"This is it. This is what we've been hoping for, don't you see?" The other monk took a step back, looked down and then started to mumble, as if he was thinking out loud. "We must place it on the altar high, send the devil to the fire. Power over men we'll have when they see it shine…when they see it shine…"

Facing Jehan, Florent commanded, "Brother, fetch the abbot now, tell him of this wondrous thing."

"Are you certain? You know the abbot doesn't like to be disturbed," Jehan said. "Why would he care? What possible use would he have for such an object, aside from selling it?"

Florent's face was turning red, and not due to the cold air. "Tell him that we'll have control of all the riches it will bring. When people come to see it, for money we will purify their souls." Florent rubbed his hands together and appeared to be lost in thought. "Their souls…" he repeated.

"I'll let him in—you fetch the abbot," Florent said. "Quickly now, go!"

೧೩೩

Abbot Ignace sat at the dinner table and scowled. The stew was watery, the bread was hard and the mead was weak. This was not a proper meal for someone of his standing. Brothers Bastien and Maximilien sat with their heads down, neither making eye contact with him. This would not do.

"Brother Maximilien," Ignace said.

The chubby monk jumped when the abbot spoke. "Yes?"

"Why do you think the Lord wanted me here at the Abbé St. Pierre, an Abbé so far away from the church's leaders?"

Maximilien's lips moved slightly, as if he was formulating what to say before he actually said it. "Because the Lord feels you are holy enough to lead these people without the constant guidance from other church officials?"

"'Guidance' is a more generous term than I would use," Ignace said. "I'd favor the word 'meddling' over it. As the Lord's chosen, I know what's best for my people—not those fools and prelates who sit in Paris and Rome."

Maximilien nodded a little. "It must be as you say, Abbot."

"And if the Lord has chosen me to lead these people, why do you think he has cursed me with such slothful monks? Monks who are such sinners that the people have stopped paying their proper tribute? Monks who continue to fail, even after I have rebuked them?"

Brother Bastien brought his head closer to his bowl of soup, seemingly to avoid Ignace's attention.

"I have been praying, Abbot, each day and night, for something to take away our sins." Maximilien took another bit of his soup and then said, "I know that once we've repented, the Lord will provide."

The abbot folded his arms and glared at Maximilien. "You must do more than pray. Prayers in and of themselves won't make the people donate properly! More severe action needs to be taken! You must—"

Ignace was interrupted when Brother Jehan barged into the room. "Forgive me, Abbot. But something wondrous has happened."

"What is it?"

"Please, just come with me.," Jehan said.

Soon the short, rotund figure of Abbot Ignace waddled across the courtyard. His golden locks bounced as he walked. Brother Jehan was close behind with Bastien and Maximilien following.

Florent had let Geoffrey and his mutt inside and had closed the gate. The peasant man bowed when the abbot approached.

"Brother Jehan says you have something to show me," Ignace said by way of greeting.

Geoffrey nodded. "Yes, Abbot. It surely is something of great value."

"Show me."

Geoffrey reached into the bag and carefully pulled out the huge diamond, which shone brightly enough to fill the courtyard with light. And there was something else—did he feel different? No, it must have been his imagination.

"Amazing…" Ignace said. Certainly this was a gift from the Lord. The abbot at once saw the possibilities of possessing such an extraordinary item.

"What a wonderful donation you have brought to me," said the abbot, holding out his hands.

Geoffrey frowned a bit and put the diamond back into the leather bag. The light and the odd sensation faded. "Donation? Yes, of course. But there is something about this object—"

"Ah, you wish for a blessing in return for the donation, do you?" Ignace asked. "Tell me, what is it your heart desires?"

There was a look of pain in Geoffrey's eyes. He bowed his head, and when he raised it again, tears were streaming down his cheeks.

"I wish to be rid of the pain I feel at the loss of my wife and sons. I felt joy for a moment recently, but it has since faded. Will you provide that? Can you take away my pain?"

Ignace looked the man over. This could pose a problem.

"I will help you, yes," Ignace said. "But first, tell me. Who else knows of this diamond?"

Geoffrey wiped the tears from his cheeks. "It's called 'the mirror of the soul.' And to answer your question, no one living knows of it but me."

"That's a strange thing to call such a diamond divine. And no one knows but you, eh?" Ignace said carefully. "One moment, please."

He stepped away from the raggedly dressed peasant and motioned for Brother Florent to follow.

When they were out of earshot of the others, Ignace said to Florent, "I know of your sins, Brother Florent. I know that before you came to the Abbé you were a common street thug. You feared being forced into the war, though you have no problem inflicting harm on others."

Florent's eyes grew wide. "How did you—"

With a wave of his hand, Ignace cut him off. "Do you forget who I am? Do you think I would not know such things?"

"Then why did you let me stay here?"

The abbot shook his head in disappointment.

"Don't you see? No, of course you don't. But take a moment to use the mind the Lord has given you."

At first Florent didn't say anything. He seemed to puzzle out what the abbot was trying to tell him. Then a look of understanding came across his face. "You brought Brother Jehan and me into the Abbé when it looked like this area might be overrun. You didn't want monks; you wanted protection."

"Very good," Ignace said. "And do you still carry your weapon with you wherever you go?"

In a swift move, Florent produced a knife from his robe's sleeve.

Motioning toward Geoffrey, Ignace said, "There is only one sure way to end that man's suffering. Do you know what it is?"

Florent nodded. "With my knife I'll kill this man; I'll send him to the Promised Land."

"And when we take the diamond," Ignace said, "we will have the future in our hands." He reached out and took Florent's hands in his. "In *our* hands."

The monk took a deep breath and approached Geoffrey with Brother Florent beside him. The peasant looked up and asked, "Will you rid me of my pain?"

Ignace nodded and motioned to Florent.

"Here is your paradise," Florent said.

A swift blow to the man's throat with Florent's sharp knife put an end to Geoffrey.

ঔ৩

Brother Jehan stood in place, stunned. As shocking as it was to see the peasant cut down, it was only made worse when the abbot instructed

Florent to kill the mutt as well. Ignace had said something about not wanting people to recognize the dog and come looking for his master. Then the abbot commanded Florent to do something horrifying. The other monk was to remove the peasant's head and then throw the head and body into the river. To what end, Jehan wasn't sure. Florent didn't seem to mind doing the bloody work, but he complained that he couldn't carry the body to the river that flowed behind the Abbé.

The abbot explained that this was the Lord's will and that the peasant had gotten his wish. If any of the monks doubted the Lord, they could leave the Abbé at that moment, though when Ignace declared it, he seemed to pass an unspoken message to Florent.

Jehan tried not to let the other monks see him weep as he dragged Geoffrey's remains, but once he got to the river's edge, he cried openly.

Though it had snowed, it hadn't yet gotten cold enough to freeze the river's normally peaceful waters. He first laid the dog in the river. Next, Geoffrey's body was dumped in. It made a bit of a splash as it hit the water. The blood from its severed neck left a crimson trail in the snow by the riverside.

All that remained was Geoffrey's head. The sightless eyes were still opened—eyes that seemed to look into Jehan's very soul.

The large monk looked around and saw that he was not being watched. Reaching into a sewn-in pocket of his robe, he removed two coins. It was an old superstition and one that the abbot would most certainly frown upon, but Brother Jehan felt he owed the man this much.

Carefully he placed one of the coins over each of Geoffrey's eyes. Then, before he put the remaining part of the man into the river, Jehan whispered, "Remember: don't pay the ferryman until he gets you to the other side."

Chapter 3

Henri and Guy stood looking at Lucien expectantly. Both of his friends were older than him, though the wide-bodied Guy was a hand span shorter. Henri was the biggest and strongest of the three, and he liked to be in charge. Lucien suspected that it was because Henri's father had died in the war, so he was the ruler of his house—at least that is what he claimed. In actuality, Henri's family was very well off and the servants did most of the work, which allowed Henri to come and go as he pleased.

"Well?" Henri asked, his arms folded.

Lucien looked at Guy, who was imitating the other boy, as he often did. His friends had found him by the side of his modest house stacking firewood. Now that he had completed that chore, he was free for the rest of the afternoon.

"I'm not sure—" Lucien started to say.

Henri threw his hands up in the air. "It's not like we are doing anything that's really wrong. It's just a bit of fun. You're always too cautious."

"But if the bartender finds us, it could get my father in trouble," Lucien said. "Isn't there another tavern we could go to?"

"No!" Henri said.

"No!" Guy echoed.

The older boy frowned a bit at Guy. He then continued, "That's where Ambre goes every night.

I've scouted the area and found a way we can climb into the rafters without being seen, but we can see everything."

"I'm not sure it's worth the risk just to look at a pretty lady," Lucien said. Ever since the summertime, Henri seemed to be overly preoccupied with the fairer sex. At the age of twelve, Lucien didn't quite see what was so important. Yes, some of the ladies were pleasant to look at, but not enough to hazard doing something stupid like Henri was suggesting.

"It's not any pretty lady—it's Ambre!" Henri said, sounding bewildered that they were even having this conversation.

Lucien frowned. "I'll tell you what. You both go and try it out if you want. If you can do it without getting caught, maybe I'll come next time."

"Bah, all right then. C'mon, Guy," Henri said.

Lucien's two friends walked off into the falling snow.

❧

Christophe dusted off his shoulders before he entered his home. Along with the snow, it had been a windy night. He removed the key from under his cloak and carefully slid it into the lock. There was a candle burning in the window—Rosette always left one there on the nights he was entertaining. He was home a bit later than normal tonight. He had stayed and sung a few extra songs to the delight of the patrons of Jourdain's tavern.

As quietly as he could, Christophe opened the lock. He didn't want to wake his wife or son.

Upon entering the sitting room that doubled as their dining room, Christophe noticed his wife, Rosette. She was sitting in her favorite rocking chair, knitting something that looked like socks. She wore the red shawl he had given her for her birthday—she always looked good in red. Even at this late hour and in the candlelight, she was stunning. He wasn't sure what he had done to be blessed with such a beautiful wife, but whatever it had been, he was grateful.

"Good evening to you, husband." She smiled.

He closed the door behind him and re-latched the lock. "And a good evening to you as well, wife. Why are you still awake?"

Her hands stopped working on the knitting. "I've been missing you, more than words can say."

"I've been gone quite a bit lately, haven't I?" Christophe admitted. He removed his cloak and took off his snow-encrusted boots.

Again, Rosette smiled. "That you have, though I understand. I hear that you're becoming more in demand at the tavern and that other tavern owners are seeking you out."

"And where have you heard that?" Christophe asked playfully.

"Oh, word gets around," she said. "Come, sit with me."

Christophe took a dining chair and placed it next to his wife. "So, my lady in red, what did Lucien do this evening?"

She turned to him, a perplexed look in her eyes. "He was here, in his room. Why do you ask?"

"We had a bit of an incident at the tavern tonight," Christophe said.

"Incident?"

"During one of my performances, a woman near the front had something land in her soup. It took us a moment to realize it was a boot."

Rosette looked at him curiously. "A boot? How would a boot fall from the sky?"

"Not from the sky," Christophe said, shaking his head. "From the rafters. It looks like two boys had found a way to climb up there. How long they had been there, I can't say. It's pretty cramped in the rafters, so I'd guess one had taken off his boots to massage his aching feet. We found out later his companion accidently knocked it over the edge."

"Was the woman hurt?"

"No, though she was a bit shaken up."

Rosette chuckled. "Ah, young boys, always making mischief of one kind or another. But what does that have to do with Lucien? As I said, he was here all night. I'm sure of it."

"Because the boys were his friends, Guy and Henri."

"Guy and Henri? Why would they hide in the rafters? To eavesdrop on your storytelling? They're over here all the time and you perform for them anytime they ask."

It was Christophe's turn to laugh. "They weren't there for me."

"Oh, then why?"

"There are a number of pretty ladies that frequent the tavern."

Rosette arched an eyebrow at Christophe. He reached out and took her hand.

He squeezed it tightly. "There are none that come close to your beauty. In fact, I dare say you've never looked so lovely as you do tonight."

She reached up with her other hand and placed it on his cheek. "It's no wonder I fell in love with you. How could a woman resist a man with such a silver tongue?"

They sat there for a moment, looking into each other's eyes. Christophe felt a warmth wash over him—a warmth of pure love for his wife. He felt a moment of inspiration hit, and softly he whispered to her, "Surely we have a love of a different world, love of the life, love of the ancient ones, love of the heart divine."

"How do you come up with such words, husband?" she asked, tears starting to form in her eyes.

"You inspire me."

"Let me try," she said.

Christophe nodded.

She pursed her lips and appeared to be deep in thought. Then she said, "These quiet moments make my day—we must never let them slip away."

"Very nice," he said. "May I use that in a song at some point in time?"

"Oh, I don't know…" she said, a hint of playfulness in her voice. "What do I get in return?"

With that, Christophe stood and offered her his hand. She set the knitting down and allowed him to help her up. He took her into his arms, then whispered in her ear, "Me."

❧

Abbott Ignace set the leather bag on the table before him. He had gathered the four monks together to let them know of his plan. They had all reacted differently to the events that had led to getting the diamond. It was no matter. He would set them all straight.

"Let me make one thing clear," Ignace said to the monks seated around the table. "We did not commit murder. We were doing the Lord's will. The old man had nothing left to live for on this earth. It was an act of mercy to let him go to his eternal reward. Brother Florent is not to be blamed, any more than you would blame his knife. He was simply the Lord's tool, doing the Lord's work."

Florent looked smug at the proclamation. Bastien's face was one of what? Envy? Maybe he thought he should have been worthy? Maximilien merely sat with his hands resting on his rather large belly, while Jehan looked a bit ill.

"Brethren, I have been inspired by the Lord. And I believe Brother Florent has been inspired as well. You see, the people have lost their way. They have forgotten the power of the Lord. They have forgotten that they need Him in their lives. They have taken their beliefs for granted, and now we have something new for them to believe in."

He stood up as tall as he could. "We have been chosen by the Lord to create a new religion—one where the people need the Lord and will do whatever we say to get the help they need."

"A new religion?" Brother Jehan asked. "Are you saying we forsake the old ways?"

Ignace felt his face turn red from anger. "No! We will not forsake what we know to be true.

"This is just the next step, don't you see? Moses was given the Ten Commandments. Jesus came and gave us new laws to follow, new things to believe in."

He pointed to the leather sack. "This! This is the next step. Just like the star that appeared at the birth of Jesus, a light in the night sky announced the arrival of such a wondrous item. Just as Jesus was born in humble surroundings, this diamond divine was found by a poor peasant man. The meaning couldn't be more clear!"

"But how will such an item bring to pass the next phase of our religion?" Brother Bastien asked.

"Ah," Ignace said, "now you are asking the right questions. Brother Florent, what are your thoughts on the matter?"

Florent grinned. "In the chapel, we have the three altars. At the altar low, people will make their donations. At the altar mid, we preach the word of the Lord. And it is on the altar high where we will place the diamond."

"So, people will need to do what? Make donations to see the diamond?" Bastien asked. "Even when we make it shine, it will only impress people for so long."

"Exactly!" Ignace said. "Brother Maximilien, what would inspire people to return?"

Maximilien frowned as he thought. "It was only through our sacrifices that we were given such a marvelous item. For others to fully receive the blessings they desire, they, too, will need to make sacrifices."

"And what kinds of sacrifices are needed?" Ignace asked, knowing the answer he already wanted to hear. "Brother Jehan? What do you think?"

The largest of the monks continued to look a bit pale.

He seemed to push whatever was bothering him aside and answered, "They would need to give up what they desire the most to prove their worth to the Lord."

Ignace nodded. "And what does man desire the most?"

"Gold," Brother Florent blurted out. "Riches. Wealth. With these things they can buy power, women—anything."

The abbot smiled. "Brethren, you have seen the light. You all know this to be the Lord's will. Therefore, let us pray for guidance on what types of blessings are to be given in exchange for different amounts of gold."

"But what of the diamond?" Brother Jehan asked.

"What of it?"

"We've not taken it from the sack since…"

It now occurred to Ignace what was bothering Brother Jehan. While he was the largest and strongest of the monks, he was also the least prone to wrath and violence. Ignace had brought him on as a monk because he was one of the most imposing men he'd seen. But looks could be deceiving, as was the case with Brother Jehan. It was no wonder the man had become a monk instead of a soldier. Yet he did make a good point. Ignace had not brought out the diamond. Why? He hadn't given much consideration to it, aside from the thought that it seemed sacrilegious to handle the object so casually. *Yes. That must be the reason.*

"It's an object of a most holy nature," Ignace

responded. "It isn't to be handled like a common rock.

It is a diamond divine, in fact, that is what we'll call it. It stays in the sack until we can prepare the altar high. It will need a fine cushion to rest upon—something purple and velvet. Brother Maximilien, go into town and commission such an item. The rest of you will retire to your rooms and begin to make a list of blessings people can earn with their donations. Go, and let the Lord guide your thoughts."

ঔৣ

"I had it all planned out—sneaking in, the place to watch, the getaway, everything! That was until Guy knocked my shoe off the rafter," Henri said.

The three young men were sitting on a rock wall, which was about waist-high off the ground. Lucien had been given a stern warning from his mother about letting his friends be bad influences on him. It upset him a little because he had always tried to be a good person, and he felt like he was being blamed for something he hadn't done. She hadn't outright banned him from seeing Henri and Guy, but she said she'd be watching.

"I told you I was sorry, Henri," Guy said glumly. "I didn't even realize you had taken your shoe off."

Lucien tried to play peacemaker. "It sounds like it was an accident."

"It was." Guy nodded his head.

Henri let out a big sigh. "Accident or not, you need to be more careful. Unlike your father, a painter, my family is well connected and I need to be concerned about my image."

Lucien thought about telling Henri that perhaps he shouldn't be going up in the rafters of an inn if he was worried about his reputation. However, Henri seemed to always know what was best and would most likely get upset if he said it.

"My father's a good painter. He has lots of people tell him that," Guy said, sounding defensive.

It was rare that Guy stood up to Henri, and it was something that Lucien thought he should do more often.

Henri smirked. "Especially the ladies, eh, Guy? I've noticed how women are drawn to him, excuse the pun."

"They like how he paints." Guy shrugged. "He can make them look real pretty on canvas."

"I think your father is an excellent painter, Guy," Lucien added. "And since your mother died when you were little, there's nothing wrong with your father courting other women."

"Courting?" Henri asked. "Is that what you call it? I'd call it—"

"That's enough, Henri," Lucien said. "Just because you are upset that you got caught, it doesn't make it all right for you to pick on Guy. You're friends, after all."

The older boy looked at Lucien and then at Guy. His scowl faded gradually. "You're right."

He stuck out his hand to Guy. "Still friends?"

Guy didn't hesitate to shake Henri's hand. "Friends."

"Great," Henri said, "now that we've put that behind us, there is something else I want to investigate."

Lucien shook his head. Henri's ideas often bordered on doing things he shouldn't do. "And what's that?" Lucien asked warily.

"I've heard from a few different townspeople of a graveyard in the hills near here," Henri said.

"So what?" Lucien asked. "There is a graveyard right by the Abbé."

Henri wagged a finger in front of Lucien's face. "Ah, ah, ah! This one is different. It is said that one of the graves has flowers on it."

Even Guy looked unimpressed by Henri's statement.

"So, you want to do what? Go off to the hills one day to see that someone left flowers on a grave?" Lucien asked.

"Bah!" Henri said. "Don't you understand? It isn't that someone left them there; the flowers are actually growing, even though it is winter."

◆

Almost lovingly, Jehan placed the velvet pillow on the altar high. It had taken more time than the abbot wanted to get the resting place of the diamond divine—several weeks, as velvet wasn't easy to come by. The first two pillows presented were rejected out of hand by the leader of the Abbé.

The monks were sworn to secrecy about the diamond until it was ready for public display. In the meantime, they had drafted a set of doctrines for their new religion. Jehan wasn't sure about the promises made or the conditions that were set forth, but the other monks were in full support of the abbot—at least outwardly, and Jehan didn't want to risk voicing his doubts to the others.

"At last," the abbot said. "We are ready. Brother Florent, since you were chosen of the Lord to be his instrument, I will allow you the honor of placing the diamond."

This seemed odd to Brother Jehan. For some reason, the abbot almost seemed reluctant to touch the diamond, though it was the center of all their new plans. They had yet to open the sack from the time Geoffrey was killed.

Brother Florent beamed with pride at the announcement. The abbot handed the leather sack to the monk.

"Brother Jehan, help me with this."

Jehan nodded. He went to reach for the bag and was overwhelmed by the sensation that he shouldn't. He fought hard against the feeling and grabbed the bottom of the sack. With Florent's hands reaching out, Jehan tilted the sack so the diamond would slide out.

The large diamond seemed to hang in midair for a moment before it landed in Florent's hands.

And then a most amazing thing happened.: nothing.

The diamond did not shine.

Chapter 4

For a moment no one spoke. Then Florent started shaking the diamond, as if doing so would make it shine. Still, no light.

"Here! Give it to me!" Ignace commanded. It seemed the abbot's reluctance to touch the diamond was overridden by his anger.

His small hands grabbed the diamond from Florent. The abbot turned the diamond this way and that, appearing to search for a way to make it shine. After several tense moments, Ignace handed the diamond to Bastien. "See if you can figure out how the old man made it work," he said through gritted teeth. He spun toward Florent. "You killed him too quickly! There has to be a way to light the diamond. And with the peasant dead, we can't ask him!"

Florent looked flustered. "Abbot, I—"

The monk was silenced when Ignace put a finger in his face. "No, no excuses. You will need to figure out how he made it look like it was shining—that is, if you want to stay in the Abbé."

"I don't see how he did it," Bastien said. The bald monk was still scrutinizing the diamond. "It must have been a trick of light somehow."

Maximilien spoke as he twisted his fingers nervously in his long beard. "Yes, that must be it. He was reluctant to give up the diamond until we promised him something in return."

The abbot's ears were turning red, something that Jehan had only seen a few times before, and it was always followed by Ignace going on a tirade. He thought he had better say something before that could happen. "Just because we haven't found a way to make it shine yet doesn't mean it isn't a gift from the Lord," Jehan said quickly before Ignace could explode in rage.

The leader of the Abbé looked at Jehan, his face now nearly as red as his ears.

"There is no denying that this diamond is special," Jehan continued. "Many reported seeing a light in the sky. Several others went in search for whatever it was, but found nothing but a deep hole in the ground. And then the old man came to the door with this diamond, claiming it to be that very object. Where would he get such a thing? I believe this is a gift from the Lord."

The words seemed to have the calming effect for which Jehan had hoped. Ignace's face was merely pink now, instead of red.

"But unless it shines, all our plans we have put together over the last few weeks will be for naught. We know it is a gift, but will the common man? I fear that if they don't see it shine, it won't be inspiring enough," Ignace said.

"Then we'll figure out a way to make it shine," Bastien said. "After all, if a poor peasant can figure it out, surely as the Lord's chosen, we can."

ଔ

The sunshine felt good on Lucien's face. It had been a hard winter so far—the harshest he could remember. After that first snowfall, the ground had been continually covered in white. Though there had been some warm days, they had never been warm enough for the snow to completely melt.

Today had been one of the nicer days. It was the warmest it had been in quite a while, so people took advantage of the sunshine and went outside. His mother had given him leave, so he was off to find his friends.

The last time he, Henri and Guy had done something together was when they had gone to see the grave with the flowers growing on it. Though Lucien had seen it with his own eyes, it was almost too strange for him to believe. He had told his mother about it, and she simply smiled and said there was probably an explanation for it, though what it was, she couldn't say. Whether she believed him or not wasn't clear to Lucien. His father was a bit more accepting of the idea, telling him that there were many wonderful things in this world he couldn't explain, but it didn't mean they weren't real.

Henri seemed to get bored of the flowered grave quickly and moved onto other ideas. His older friend's latest idea involved setting up a merchant's stand across from where Ambre sold her wares. From there, he could watch her throughout the day. However, when it came to the details of what to sell and that Henri would have to stand in one place most of the day, he dismissed it and started working on his next plan.

After walking around the town for a little while, he found Guy by the Abbé. His stout friend held a raised hand to his forehead, shading his eyes from the sun.

"What are you looking at?" Lucien asked when he was close enough.

Guy turned and smiled. "Something's happening on the chapel's roof."

"What do you mean?"

"Look." Guy pointed.

A couple of the monks were on the roof of the Abbé's tallest building. What they were doing, Lucien couldn't tell.

"They probably have a leak from all the snow we've had and are fixing it," Lucien said.

Guy looked doubtful. "Why would the monks fix their own roof?"

"Well," Lucien said, "before he became a monk, Brother Bastien was quite the crafter, or so my father tells me. Maybe the abbot is having them fix it as some sort of penance."

"Hmmm. Maybe," Guy conceded.

Lucien bent down and scooped up a handful of snow and packed it into a ball. "It's too nice of a day to stand here and watch the monks work. Where's Henri?"

Guy was still staring at the Abbé, oblivious to Lucien's actions. "He ran off with Tatienne. I think they went to the other side of the river. You know, to be alone. He says being with her makes him warm."

"Ha! I'll bet it does." Lucien laughed. "I have an idea. Let's go find him and cool him off, shall we?"

Still peering up at the monks working, Guy asked, "And how would we do that?"

Lucien's answer was to hold up a perfectly made snowball.

଄଄

The sun was starting to set and they had yet to find Henri. They were about to give up and go home when they heard Henri call out to *them*. He was hiding behind a bush on the other side of the river with only his head visible.

"Lucien! Guy! I need your help!" Henri shouted.

The two friends looked at each other and smiled. "Sure!" Guy responded. "We'll help you!"

With that, the boys unleashed a barrage of snowballs at their friend.

"Stop! Please, stop!" Henri begged after several of the projectiles found their mark.

Lucien was laughing so hard he almost couldn't shout back, but he regained his composure enough to say, "Give us a good reason to stop, and we'll consider it!"

Henri's response was to come out from behind the bush.

He was completely naked.

Lucien sighed. *What had Henri gotten himself into now?* "Where are your clothes?" Lucien shouted.

Henri was stomping and jumping around in the snow, most likely to try to keep warm. "It doesn't matter! Just get me a cloak and some boots. I don't fancy spending a night on the river!"

"Fine! Stay put—we'll be right there!"

"Lucien! Guy! I'm counting on you!" Henri cried out from the other side of the river.

Lucien turned to Guy. "I'm going to go over there and give him my cloak. You run and get him some boots. We'll meet you by the bridge, all right?"

Guy nodded and then ran off toward the town.

"Head to the bridge; I'll meet you there!" Lucien shouted.

Henri looked around, appearing nervous, but then seemed to be resigned to the fact that being seen naked was better than freezing.

When the two met up on the far side of the bridge, Henri was hiding behind a tree, several paces away. Henri was visibly shaking from exposure to the cold. Lucien removed his cloak and offered it to his friend. "Guy will be here soon with the boots. We need to get you inside before parts of you turn black and fall off."

Henri looked down, then frowned, which seemed difficult to do since his teeth were chattering. He grabbed the cloak and quickly put it on, then stepped out from behind the tree.

Lucien sighed. "You're always getting yourself into trouble. Some things never change. What happened this time?"

"It started out innocently enough," Henri said. "Tatienne and I went for a walk. After we were alone, she dared me to take a swim in the water. I asked her what I'd get in return. She smiled and said it would be a surprise."

"You went into *that*?" Lucien pointed at the river that had thawed just the previous week.

"You know I can't refuse a pretty face," Henri said, making it sound like a curse.

Lucien rolled his eyes. "So you took off all your clothes and went into the river."

"Yes."

"And?"

Henri paused before answering. "After I went

in, Tatienne gathered up my clothes. She told me how she had spotted me kissing Désirée. She got rather upset. Now my clothes and the lady are well out of sight. Happy now?"

"Ah, Henri, what were you thinking?"

The older boy shrugged. "Like I said, I can't refuse a pretty face."

ଓଃ

"Perhaps we'll open on the Sabbath," Didier announced.

Christophe's stomach tightened at the comment. He already worked six days a week at the store, and the Sabbath was the one day he could spend with his family. "May I ask why?"

The store owner made a rude noise. "The monks at the Abbé St. Pierre haven't held services for nearly three months. People are just wandering the streets on the Sabbath as it is. If we were open, and no one else was, we would make a hefty profit."

Christophe thought how to counter his boss's argument in a way that it wouldn't make him mad. He finally said, "As I hear it, the abbot has been sick, but is recovering. Soon they'll have services again. I'm not sure he would look favorably upon the store being open on the Sabbath."

Didier laughed. "Ignace doesn't hold as much power as he once did. Yes, at one point people were flocking to him for guidance during the war, but not anymore.

"And he hasn't helped his own cause by turning everyone away."

"Well, if he's been ill," Christophe suggested,

"that would explain why he's not allowing people into the Abbé."

"Oh no, no, no," Didier said. "That's not it."

Christophe rested his elbows on the counter before him. Though it was the day before the Sabbath, there had been very few customers. He preferred it when his boss went hunting and left him to run the shop. When Didier was here, he was constantly nitpicking everything that Christophe did—to the point where he couldn't be as productive. Sadly, today was one of those days.

"Then why do you think he's been turning people away?" Christophe asked.

Didier gave Christophe a look one would give if someone asked why fire was hot. "It's because he's become too pious. He's too good for the rest of us. Our problems are beneath him."

What Didier was claiming made a certain type of sense, though Christophe had always found comfort in the chapel's walls—walls he hadn't entered in quite some time due to the claimed illness of the abbot. What had been once walls of comfort had now become walls of silence.

"Be that as it may," Christophe said carefully, "if you opened the store on the Sabbath, it would just be a matter of time before other owners would do the same.

"The abbot will eventually return to good health, or the church will replace him. In either case, I'm sure the church would condemn such an action."

Didier didn't look convinced. "The church is losing its influence. I sense it. I'm betting the other merchants sense it too. Some of my traders have hinted as much themselves."

This last statement bothered Christophe. To Didier, the church's power was in the hands of its leaders. But the church wasn't made by man; it was established by a higher power—the world's creator. Going against the church wasn't defying man; it was defying God.

"You are the boss, of course," Christophe said, keeping his tone neutral. "However, I still think we will hear something from the Abbé soon. If the abbot does regain his power, a power you feel he is losing, he would most likely condemn having the store open on the Sabbath. It could cause the store to actually lose money in the long run."

Didier eyed Christophe for a moment. He didn't look happy. Finally, he harrumphed and said, "Fine! I'll have to find a different way to make more money."

☙❧

"Are you sure I can't help on the roof?" Brother Jehan asked.

Abbot Ignace scowled. "As big as you are, you'd probably make a hole."

Jehan found this ironic since that is exactly what Brothers Bastien and Florent had done. Directly above the altar high they had cut out a hole. It wasn't terribly large, and it wasn't visible unless you knew exactly where to look.

Both he and the abbot looked up at where Bastien and Florent were working.

Brother Maximilien was watching the front gate, something Jehan would have been happy to do

instead of standing inside the chapel with the abbot.

"This had better work," Ignace grumbled.

Jehan didn't respond. Several things had been tried to make the diamond appear like it was shining. However, all the different methods they tried with candles and fire were uninspiring. It was then that Brother Bastien had come up with the idea of using the light of the sun.

"I've heard rumors from the townspeople," Jehan said, trying to distract the abbot from the awkward silence between them.

"What rumors are those?" Ignace asked, still staring at the hole in the roof where the monks were working.

"There is talk that you have died and we are trying to keep it a secret," Jehan said.

This was enough to get Ignace's attention. "Who has said such things?"

"In the market, I hear things when I'm buying supplies for our meals. I think people say these rumors just loud enough that I can hear them, but they pretend to be talking to someone else at the time. I believe they want me to know they suspect the story of your long illness to be untrue."

"A lie?" the abbot said. "I would not break the ninth commandment! We simply told the towns-people that no more services would be held until I was able to do so. They drew their own conclusions."

"Can we at least let them know you are well, and that we will be holding services again soon?"

"Ah, you're afraid that we will run out of money, is that it?"

"That's part of it, yes," Jehan admitted. The

treasury was dangerously low—something that should have caused the abbot to be very upset, but instead, Ignace seemed almost obsessed with the diamond.

"Don't fool yourself," Ignace said. "That's *exactly* it. I know we are almost out of money and food storage. But I promise you this, when the light of the diamond divine shines, we'll have wealth and power we can now only dream of having. And let me reassure you, it's a matter of when, and not if. Just last night I had a vision about—"

"We're ready!" shouted Brother Bastien from above, interrupting the abbot.

Ignace rubbed his hands together. "Position the mirror!"

As Jehan understood it, Brother Bastien had placed a number of highly reflective surfaces in a circular area around the hole. Then, right above the hole was the most expensive mirror that could be found in the surrounding area. This mirror was on a hinge that could spin in several directions, so no matter where the sun was in the sky, the mirror could be positioned to reflect a beam of sunshine directly toward the diamond.

For a moment nothing happened. Then a shaft of sunlight shone through the hole in the roof and onto the large gem. The effect was breathtaking. It appeared that the diamond was shining, with tiny rainbows reflecting off its surface. Yet, despite being visually stunning, there was a warmth missing that Jehan had felt when the old man had held the diamond.

"It's perfect…" Ignace said, the awe in his voice unmistakable.

"It looks as if the diamond divine is sending the light skyward instead of the other way around. Yes, we have been blessed. The man who brought us the diamond divine must have done something similar to make it shine."

Jehan thought better than to remind the abbot that the peasant had come after the sun had set.

The short abbot grabbed Jehan by both arms. He looked up at the larger man. "You see, don't you, Brother? It's not the light that is special, it's the diamond divine. But people are often blind to the Lord's gifts. This will help them see." The abbot then smiled. "Sound the chapel bells. The time of the new religion has arrived."

Chapter 5

The chapel was full. There were even people standing along the back wall. Ignace allowed himself a secret smile before he went to the altar mid. He stood just inside his private room, listening to the comments people made as they entered and sat on the pews. "I heard the chapel bells," one man said. "I'd almost forgotten what they sounded like."

Another man said, "I wonder who will be leading the services. I heard that Abbot Ignace is dead." And yet the third comment was the one he was most interested in. "What's up there on the altar high? I can't tell; it's covered by some sort of purple cloth."

So, someone had noticed the diamond divine, even though it was covered. *Excellent.* It would make its unveiling that much more effective. In addition, he'd had a powerful dream the night before. It could have been nothing less than a vision from the Lord. He didn't believe it was coincidence that he had the dream the night before this most important service. The Lord wanted him to share the message.

Ignace looked over his robe—newly created out of the same fabric that covered the diamond. It wasn't by chance; Ignace wanted people to see a direct connection between him and the holy object. Convinced all was in place, he opened the door fully and then walked solemnly toward the altar mid.

Any whispers from the parishioners came to an abrupt end when Ignace made his entrance. He methodically climbed the stairs to the altar mid, and upon reaching it, placed his hands on either side of the pulpit which sat atop the altar.

"It has been far too long since we have met," Ignace said as his introduction, trying to sound humble. "But as the good Lord said, patience is a virtue. You see, I have been doing the Lord's work which has kept me from holding services. I am deeply sorry as I know this has been hard for you not to be able to come to the chapel and worship. However, as you will see, it will be worth it. My good people, I have had a vision most wonderful—a vision from the risen Lord."

Ignace noticed the complete attention of everyone in the chapel.

"In my vision, I was lost in the dark and fear was in my heart. The only things around me were the forest and the rain. And then, there was a flash of light! I don't know how I knew, but I understood I must be getting near St. Peter's Gate!"

He saw a few women bring their hands to their chests out of shock at this statement. *Splendid.*

"I went through the door and there standing in the hall was an old man with a beard of shining white," Ignace said, his voice getting slightly louder. "His angelic voice spoke a message to me—a message I was to share with all those who would hear."

Leaning forward and staring intently at the people in the congregation, he said, "Nobody will get through—nobody! Not even I, the abbot. Nobody will escape the judgment day. Heaven is only there for the ones who satisfy them at St. Peter's Gate!

"But how? How do we meet the requirements set upon us? Many of you come here on the Sabbath, worship for the short time you are here, and then the rest of the week, you do as you please. This is unacceptable. The Lord requires more from you. And in my vision, I asked the same question that is certainly on all of your minds at this moment. 'What must I do?'"

People were nodding their heads in agreement, and some even appeared to be flushed and pale from guilt. *Wonderful.*

"I was told in my vision that a most holy object would save us. Not unlike when Moses received the Ten Commandments, or when Noah was given the knowledge that he should build an ark, I was given a charge from the Lord. That charge was to save as many as I could—those willing to make sufficient sacrifices to please them at St. Peter's Gate.

"That holy object is here now with us in this very chapel." Ignace motioned to the altar high. People's eyes swept upward.

Ignace stepped back from the altar mid, and climbed the stone steps that led to the altar high. Upon reaching the top, he said, "What I'm about to reveal is an object given to me by the Lord. From its power, your sins, past, present and future, can be absolved—but only to those willing to make sacrifices. If you are not willing to do what is asked, you must leave now."

No one in the room made any attempt to leave. *Superb.*

"I see you are all truly followers of the Lord,"

Ignace said. "Now, behold! The diamond divine!"

Ignace ceremoniously removed the cloth covering the precious gem, careful not to touch it. There were gasps from the crowd, and some slight murmuring.

"You may wonder what this object is and what it does," Ignace said. "In order to demonstrate, I need someone willing to make a sacrifice. This sacrifice is symbolic of our worldly possessions. The first to place ten gold coins on the altar low will receive the primary blessing. Which is what, you may ask? It is this, you will receive forgiveness of all your previous sins."

At first, no one moved. Ten gold coins was a large amount of money—an amount very few could afford to carry with them. Of course, Ignace knew that. It had to be a large sum to truly inspire the people.

A wealthy merchant stood up. He owned several farms and employed dozens of people in the surrounding area. All eyes in the room watched as he stepped forward, reached into his coin purse and then deliberately placed the ten coins on the altar low.

"Come forward, my son," Ignace instructed, pointing to a place near the altar high that would allow him to place one hand on the man's head, while at the same time, he could touch the diamond with his other hand. The merchant did as instructed.

Ignace looked up and could see that next to the hole in the roof was a strip of yellow cloth, just big enough to spot if you knew where to look.

The yellow cloth was the sign from Brother Bastien that the mirrors were positioned properly and that they were listening for his command.

"You will be blessed for your sacrifice," Ignace said to the merchant. He put his left hand on the man's head. Then in a loud voice, the abbot chanted, "Lucifer ex inferno clamat. Ne nos inducat in tentationem!"

Ignace then placed his hand on the back of the diamond, hidden from view from the rest of the congregation. At that moment, Brother Bastien opened the hole in the roof, letting the light in. The effect was exactly what Ignace had hoped. The chapel filled with light that appeared to come from the diamond.

People fell to their knees, clutched their hands together, and begged for the chance to be next.

Perfect.

ꕥ

Rosette frowned, something she rarely did. In fact, Christophe couldn't recall the last time his wife had done so.

"What's bothering you, dear?" he asked.

They were sitting at the table after their evening meal. Lucien had already gone to his room, and this was the time when he and Rosette spoke about their plans for the upcoming week. She had been cheery enough during supper, but as soon as their son left, she appeared to be deep in thought—and whatever she was thinking about was making her frown.

She looked up from her empty plate. "The abbot and, oh what did he call it? The diamond divine. I'm not sure how I feel about it."

"The people in town seemed very impressed.

There were many standing in line to make appointments to receive blessings," Christophe said.

"But, dear husband, what do you think?"

Christophe thought a moment before he spoke. "I believe there are a great many things I don't know. The light coming from the diamond divine was breathtaking. I can't imagine an object like that being made by man."

"I'll agree to that. It certainly was something to behold," she said. "However, it feels, oh, wrong somehow, for people to pay for blessings and forgiveness."

"The abbot said they weren't payments—they were sacrifices. You'll have to admit that it is quite a sacrifice to donate that much gold to the church."

Rosette snapped her fingers. "And that's what's bothering me. There are set prices for different blessings or absolutions of sins. And if a person can't pay in gold, the abbot will assign the items donated a price value. The sacrifices aren't based on what a person earns. In the end, I fear only the rich will be able to buy their way into heaven."

"I see how you can look at it that way," Christophe said. He was growing uncomfortable with the conversation.

"But you don't agree with me, do you?"

He gave his wife his warmest smile. "I'll be honest. I'm not sure *how* I feel. All of this is so new. This may certainly be a remarkable gift from God. I, for one, am going to hold judgment until we can save up for a blessing and see for ourselves."

"And which blessing are you going to choose? There was certainly a long list." Rosette asked.

"Even if you were to save all you could for the

rest of your life," she continued, "you couldn't pay for an assured passage through St. Peter's Gate."

"The abbot said it wasn't the only way to get into heaven—just the most certain," Christophe pointed out. "As for which blessing, it wouldn't be for me. It would be for you."

Rosette seemed startled. "Oh?"

He reached across the table to take her hand. She gave it. "I would buy you the blessing of good health. Each year, I fear for you when winter comes. It seems the cold is harder on you as we get older."

"My dear husband." She smiled for the first time since the meal was finished. "I should have known you would think of me first."

"You are the reason for all I do," he said. "I can't begin to tell you what you mean to me."

Rosette's eyes began to tear up. "I'm sure with that silver tongue of yours, you could find a way."

"Then that's what I'll do," he said. "I'll write you a love song. One just for you."

❧

The son and the father stood side by side in the line of people waiting to get into the Abbé St. Pierre.

"Who did you say was getting blessed, Father?" Lucien asked.

"I don't know his name. I just know he is from Bordeaux and is very wealthy."

Lucien scratched his nose. "And what's so special about this blessing?"

Christophe looked down at his son. "He's to be the first person blessed with the promise of eternal life."

"And how's this going to be any different from the other blessings we've witnessed?" Lucien asked.

That was an interesting question, and one that Rosette had asked as well. Perhaps his wife had been expressing her ever-growing doubts about the diamond divine to Lucien. In fact, after the first few blessings, Rosette hadn't attended any more of them. This concerned Christophe. But when his wife made up her mind about something, it was difficult, if not impossible, to sway her.

"Aside from this being the first time this particular blessing will be performed, the abbot is said to announce something today," Christophe replied.

"Like what?"

"I don't know." He was finding it more difficult to be patient.

Lucien didn't respond verbally. Instead, he chewed on his lower lip, something he had picked up from his mother—meaning he was thinking about something.

"All right, Lucien, out with it. What's on your mind?"

His son shrugged. "It just seems like this is an odd place for such a miraculous event to happen. Why not Paris? Or Rome? After all, nothing ever happens around here—at least until now."

"Why was Jesus born in Bethlehem instead of Jerusalem?" Christophe countered. "It's often from humble beginnings that such wondrous things come to pass."

Lucien sighed. "Now you are just repeating what the abbot said."

He had heard enough. Christophe took his son

by the shoulders and looked into his eyes. "Lucien, there are a great number of things in the world we can't explain. Can you explain the flowers that grow on the grave in the hills even during winter? I can't. There is something special about this diamond. I know it. Please, son, show some faith."

The boy didn't move for a drawn-out moment, but then his countenance softened. "All my life you've filled my head with fantastic stories of faraway places. I love hearing your tales. I enjoy daydreaming and like to pretend to be in your stories. But they've always been just that: stories. To have something so…real, here, in our town is, oh, I don't know…it almost seems like something out of one of your stories."

Christophe knelt down by his son and considered him carefully. "When you were younger, you believed my stories were true. What changed?"

"I'm not sure," Lucien said. "I can't pinpoint a time when I realized they weren't real."

"It's because you are getting older and starting to recognize some of the realities of life around us. But don't you see? That's *why* I make up and tell these stories—to keep me believing in things that could be."

Lucien frowned. "Like the diamond divine?"

"Yes, like the diamond divine," Christophe said. He stood up. "So, are you telling me that you're too old to hear my stories, even the ones you ask me to tell you over and over?"

His son shook his head. "I'll never grow tired of hearing them. I really enjoy it when you take me back to the places I've never been."

ଓଃ୬ଽ

Ignace smiled at his own reflection. He liked how the purple robe complimented his golden curls. In a word, he simply looked heavenly. And why not? He had been chosen to bring the Lord's new religion to the world. He was doing good, and he was being blessed for it—and justly so.

Brother Maximilien had asked to see him before today's services. That man was so needy. It seemed he was always seeking an audience with the abbot since the diamond divine had been revealed to the people—unless, of course, Maximilien was eating. It was the one thing that seemed to keep the man from pestering him with little details that the brother should just take care of on his own.

"Abbot, we simply can't keep up with the demand for blessings," Brother Maximilien stated once he had been let into the abbot's chambers. "And since we can only do them on sunny days, we are getting further behind. There were some people who were rather upset that they got bumped down the list so that we could bless the man from Bordeaux today."

Ignace shook his head. "Oh, Brother Maximilien. Why must you tell me things I already know? Do you think me blind and deaf?"

"Of course not!" Maximilien's face turned nearly as white as his beard. "I mean no disrespect! It's just that—"

The overweight monk was silenced with a wave of Ignace's hand. "I inquired of the Lord what to do. I received another vision."

Ignace found that more and more when he was

faced with questions or problems, he would think about them and an answer would pop into his head. Because he was doing the Lord's work, these ideas could be nothing else but visions.

Understanding came to Maximilien's eyes. "Ah, this is the announcement you are making today?"

"It is."

"Forgive me, Abbot." Maximilien bowed his head. "I should have more faith."

Ignace nodded. "Yes, you should."

଼

Christophe had saved up nearly enough coin to donate to the church for his wife's blessing of health. Granted, he had had to spend a few extra nights at the tavern telling stories, and even though she hadn't spoken her opinion verbally, he could sense she wasn't happy with his absence. But didn't she know he was doing this for her? After he had enough money, he would spend more time at home. She would then see it was worth it.

Recently, the abbot had made it a point that regular attendance was required to stay on the list to be blessed. Granted, the man from Bordeaux hadn't been a regular attendee—in fact, he had made this trip to the Abbé St. Pierre solely for the singular blessing he was getting today. To Rosette, it seemed like a contradiction, and she stated as such. However, Christophe decided to take it on faith.

He and Lucien had sat down in the chapel a good while previously. Even though there were open pews ahead of them, they had been directed to sit at their current location by Brother Florent.

As the chapel began to fill, Christophe noticed that the wealthy people in town were given seats closer to the altars. Didier, his employer, was there with his wife—they were on the second row. The front row was occupied by a group who must have been the man from Bordeaux and his entourage. Christophe didn't recognize them, and they were all dressed in fine clothes.

Once the chapel was filled, the abbot entered and took his place at the altar mid. "Welcome all to the Abbé St. Pierre," the abbot said. "It is truly a blessing from the Lord that we are able to witness a miracle today. For the first time, we will be able to see someone receiving the promise of eternal life!"

Christophe noticed that everyone, even Lucien, was engrossed by the abbot.

"To mark this special occasion, the Lord has bestowed upon me another vision," the abbot continued. "As is evident by our esteemed guest from Bordeaux, word is spreading about the wondrous diamond divine. To that end, I inquired of the Lord how I could possibly meet all the requests for blessings. This vision has given me the answers!"

There wasn't a sound in the room as everyone anxiously waited for what the abbot was to reveal.

"In order to receive blessings from the diamond divine, you must pledge yourself to His new religion by officially joining the congregation. The Lord has set out certain requirements in order for people to be counted among His followers. As in my previous vision, these requirements are reflective of sacrifices you are expected to make. I've written down what the Lord revealed to me, which I'll share with you now."

The abbot held up a parchment and in a commanding voice read, "To be counted among the Lord's chosen, each member must donate, or arrange to donate, fresh produce daily to the Abbé. Members will abstain from meat, poultry and fish three days a week, and on those days, will deliver what was to have been eaten to the Abbé. In the case of someone like our esteemed guest from Bordeaux, he would make arrangements for someone local to donate these items."

Christophe felt a sense of alarm. While he ensured that his family never went hungry, it was often a struggle to do so. In order to meet these new requirements, his family would have to go hungry some days. Or maybe if just he, himself, were to skip the meals it would be enough. The abbot said sacrifices would have to be made, and this certainly would be a big one.

"On the Sabbath, as well as other days as the Lord chooses to reveal," the abbot continued, "women must wear specially blessed shoes and men will be required to wear specially blessed gloves of a certain color and style."

Blessed clothing? Where would I get such things? Christophe wondered.

As if the abbot was reading his mind, the rotund leader of the monks said, "Of course, these items will be available for purchase here at the Monastery shortly. In addition…"

The list went on and on, and with each passing requirement, Christophe realized he would be unable to meet these new demands. He thought of ways he could earn more money—he could spend more time in the tavern, or perhaps see if other taverns would take him in on different nights. He could possibly ask Didier for a higher wage, though he was pretty sure that his boss wouldn't be agreeable to sparing any extra coin.

He had been so close to getting Rosette a blessing of health. His heart felt heavy in his chest. Perhaps he wasn't worthy enough to be among the chosen. Had he done something in his life to bring this on himself? It must have been something. After all, Didier always said the Lord blessed the worthy with whatever their hearts desired. Maybe if he did some soul searching, he could find ways to be a better man—he could find a way to become worthy. Alas, that time was not now.

"Anyone unwilling to make such sacrifices must leave at once," the abbot concluded, snapping Christophe out of his introspection. Reluctantly he stood, along with most of the people in the back rows, and departed.

Chapter 6

Didier held up the finely sewn gloves so that Christophe could see them. They appeared to be made of high quality leather, with some type of religious symbols etched into the palms. "Finer craftsmanship, I've not seen." Didier gloated over his new gloves. "Wouldn't you agree?"

Christophe stood behind the counter of Didier's store and nodded in response.

"Oh, do speak up, Christophe! Or has the devil got your tongue?" Didier laughed at his own joke.

Ever since the formation of the new congregation, it seemed Didier had done all he could to be counted among the followers. He took great pride in that fact, something he taunted Christophe with often. Once, Christophe had mentioned that he needed to become worthy so that he, too, could become a member. It had been a mistake, as Didier then began to tease him about how Christophe must have let the devil into his heart at some point in time.

"They're very nice," Christophe said quietly, not meeting his employer's eyes.

"Very nice?" Didier scoffed. "Very nice, you say? How about magnificent, or glorious, or even marvelous? But perhaps the devil has dimmed your sight as well. Ah, no matter. *I* can appreciate them, as can the rest of the Lord's chosen. And do you know another reason they are of such great value?"

Christophe simply shook his head.

"These gloves, Christophe, cost me as much money as you make during a season. Others may have balked at the price, but it is worth it to be in the Lord's good graces. Speaking of which, it's a good thing you weren't able to convince me to keep the store open on the Sabbath. Though I don't blame you, of course. I know that your choices are influenced by the devil. But no fear, I'll be here for you. Part of the burden placed upon the Lord's chosen is to help the less fortunate."

"And what help do you offer me?" Christophe hoped maybe Didier would be willing to increase his wages.

Didier grinned. "Ah, that is the first step. Admitting you need help." The store owner motioned around his establishment. "We will be very busy soon. Word is spreading around the region of the diamond divine, bringing more visitors to our town. I've arranged to ship in more items from our suppliers. Here's how I'm going to help you: starting after our next delivery, you will be able to earn more coin as long as you sell a certain number of items each day."

For the first time since he had been ushered out of the monastery, Christophe felt a stirring of hope. Perhaps his prayers had been heard and this was God's answer.

"Now, keep in mind that in order for me to pay you more, and also to fulfill my obligations to the church, we'll need to sell more than in the past.

"Therefore, you will need to stay each day until you've sold what is required."

The spark of hope started to dim. "And how much am I to sell each day?" Christophe asked.

Didier told him. And it was nearly double what was sold on a normal day.

"Now, now," Didier said. "I can see you are worried. But remember, we'll have more items coming in and more customers, especially when visitors are informed I'm one of the Lord's chosen."

"I'm not sure I can meet those demands," Christophe admitted.

"It's the devil putting those doubts in your head," Didier said piously. "But fear not. I'm not without mercy. If you don't sell the required amount on a given day, you can always make up for it the next day."

"And what if I sell more than required on a given day? Can that count toward the next day?"

"Ah, you don't see, do you? In order for you to make the extra coin I'm offering, you need to sell more than the daily requirement. I'll pay you an extra coin for every additional twenty coins you earn the store on a given day. See how the Lord is allowing me to bless you?"

Christophe felt his heart beating faster in his chest. He had been praying for a way to earn more money, and it seemed that God had offered him a chance, but the task seemed almost impossible.

"And what if I fail to sell as you have asked?"

Didier's self-righteous expression changed to one that Christophe was more familiar with—loathing.

"Then I'll find someone who can."

ഗ്ദ

Brothers Maximilien, Florent and Jehan sat before the abbot as he paced back and forth. Brother Bastien was on the roof, adjusting the mirror for the day's services. Jehan wondered what this meeting could be about. The donations were flooding in, and the monks had never eaten so well nor had as much money in their coffers as they did now.

"Brethren, I have received some disturbing news from the town," Ignace said.

Maximilien twisted his fingers in his beard, a sign that he was anxious. "And what news is that?"

The abbot stopped and looked at his monks. "There are several…establishments that have opened on the outskirts of our ever-expanding town. They have taken up residence in some of the old buildings that were abandoned during the war. They claim to be taverns, though there is an abundance of barmaids employed, and their clients seem to be men who often make short but frequent visits."

Brother Jehan had heard rumors of such places. He had even heard gossip of Florent visiting them; perhaps that was where the abbot was getting his information.

"But aren't the owners of these taverns members of the church and some of our larger donors?" Maximilien asked.

Ignace nodded. "That they are."

"Is there any proof of what you are suggesting?" Maximilien continued.

The abbot motioned to Florent. "Actually, I sent Brother Florent to investigate."

Ah, Jehan thought.

"They're selling romantic encounters," Florent reported. "But it isn't that simple."

The abbot clasped his hands together in a solemn gesture. "Many, if not most, of the men who go there are church members—members who will pay for a remission of their sins at the next possible opportunity."

As usual, Jehan kept quiet and observed the reactions of the men around him. Maximilien looked disturbed, while Florent appeared smug.

Maximilien, who tended to lean toward the old ways more than the other monks, spoke up. "So, you say they are sinning on purpose with the intention of being absolved later?"

"Precisely," Ignace responded.

"And the owners of these places are being forgiven of their sins as well?" Maximilien asked.

Ignace looked indignant. "The diamond divine does not ask what sins are committed. Through it, all sins are absolved. You should know that—or are you beginning to lose your faith?"

The fat monk shook his head, causing his snowy beard to swish back and forth. "No, I'm not losing my faith. I'm merely concerned."

"Concerned about what?" Florent interrupted. "As long as they make donations, they are forgiven. It's not for us to judge."

"What if they die before receiving forgiveness through the diamond divine?" Maximilien asked.

"Then they would be damned," Florent said.

The abbot nodded. "Brother Florent is right."

"But do the members realize that?" Maximilien asked.

For a moment, the abbot said nothing. He then

looked up, his eyes appearing to glaze over. The monks looked at each other, wondering what was happening. Brother Jehan was about to stand up to see if the abbot was all right when Ignace's head snapped down.

"Brethren," Ignace said solemnly, "I have just received another vision from the Lord."

Jehan found himself holding his breath while he waited for this new revelation.

"The Lord has been waiting for us to come to this very conclusion so that we could learn from it. He doesn't want any of His congregation to be damned, but at the same time, we can't deny any of His followers the blessings of the diamond divine. To be truly safe, people should pay for an absolution for their sins in advance."

"I see the wisdom in that, Abbot," Maximilien said. "However, the donations required for future forgiveness are quite a bit higher. I'm not sure if fear alone that something *might* happen will be enough to inspire them."

"Agreed." Ignace pointed to Florent. "That's why in my vision I was to instruct Brother Florent that he must once again be the Lord's instrument."

Brother Jehan felt his body tense up as the abbot continued. "Brother Florent, you are to follow a church member as he leaves one of these establishments.

"In a quiet place, you will take his life so that others may be spared his fate. Be sure to once again remove his head and place his body in the river."

"It will be as you say." Florent sounded eager.

"Brother Jehan, you will help Brother Florent with the body."

Jehan simply nodded. He didn't want to do this, but he also didn't want to upset the abbot. He feared if he did, he might become the next person Florent was asked to eradicate.

☙❧

"Who are you going to pick?" Jehan asked.

He couldn't see Florent's face; they were deep in the shadows of a building adjacent to one of the taverns known for serving more than drinks to its customers.

"Does it really matter to you?" Florent responded. "All you've been asked to do is dispose of the body. Just stay here, out of the way and out of sight, until I come for you."

The cold night air made Jehan want to move around to stay warm, but Florent insisted they stay as quiet as possible.

Over time, several men emerged from the tavern. Jehan thought he recognized at least a few of them who were part of the new congregation, yet Florent didn't leave to follow them.

Then, finally, a man with long, flowing hair exited the building, tripping a bit as he left. Florent stealthily slipped into the night to follow the man. Jehan was pretty sure the man was Absolon, one of the tailors in the town. He was known for his good looks and his lengthy mane.

Absolon was headed toward the street when Jehan heard Florent call out to the man, quietly, but loud enough to get his attention.

The tailor seemed to have had more than a few drinks because he staggered as he walked.

"Who goes there?" Absolon slurred.

"An old acquaintance," Florent responded. "I have something for you."

Slowly and haphazardly the drunken man walked to where Florent was waiting for him behind the adjacent building.

"Oh?" Absolon hiccupped. "What's you got then?"

"Come to me and you'll see."

Though Jehan could hear them, he couldn't see the two men once Absolon turned the corner and went behind the building.

"Hey! I know you!" Absolon said. "You're one of those monks at the Abbé, aren't you? What are you doing out here? And what do you have for me?"

Jehan strained to hear Florent's next words, as they were spoken quietly. "Absolon, what have you been doing in there?"

"Ah, you know, having a drink, or two, or three…"

"What else?" Florent demanded.

"What else do you think? A lone man in a tavern full of beautiful women? Thanks to the diamond divine, I've been having all sorts of fun. You should take word back to the abbot of my thanks."

"So, have you donated to absolve you of the sins you committed tonight?" Florent asked.

Absolon made a sound that was a mixture of a burp and a laugh. "Now, don'tcha get it? I make a donation every few weeks or so to be forgiven of all my past sins. In between blessings, I have as much fun as I can. What a great new religion Ignace has set up! You're lucky to be one of his monks. I hear you're living quite the luxurious life yourself."

"I wasn't always a monk." Florent's voice took on a harder edge. "But I'm not surprised you don't remember. I was beneath you even noticing me."

There was a drawn-out silence for a moment. Jehan wondered if Florent had done the deed and was about to move toward their voices when Absolon said, "Wait. Yes, there is something familiar about you. What is it now?"

"Before I was a monk, I was a butcher's apprentice. My mentor, Viande, and you got into a fight over the price of animal skins he sold you. So, instead of coming to an agreement, you spread lies of him being a cheat and selling diseased meat. So convincing were you that Viande went out of business. He became so distraught that he hung himself, and in the process left me without a profession. I had to turn to live in the streets."

Absolon laughed again, this time a bit too loudly for Jehan's comfort. "Oh! That's right! You were that little runt that Viande took into his house after your parents were killed in the war. But things turned out well for you, didn't they? After all, you're a monk and living well now. But enough. You said you had something for me; what is it?"

Jehan heard what he assumed was Absolon being stabbed.

It sounded like several blows, followed by the tearing of flesh. Even though Jehan couldn't see anything, what he envisioned in his mind's eye made him sick to his stomach.

"Come! Now!" Florent hissed in the darkness.

Jehan took a deep breath and then went behind

the building, looking around first to make sure he wouldn't be seen. In the dim glow of the starry night, Jehan could see Florent kneeling down, his hands covered in blood. On the ground next to him was the headless body of what used to be Absolon.

"Are you all right, Brother Florent?" Jehan whispered.

The other monk stood up and said, "Of course. I was doing the Lord's work and was given a blessing by the abbot for absolution of my sins for tonight. I am spotless before the Lord. Certainly you received the same blessing as well?"

Jehan didn't respond at first. It hadn't even occurred to him to ask the abbot for such a blessing. When Florent noticed Jehan's hesitation, he pulled out the knife from the folds in his robe and looked dangerously at Jehan.

"I wasn't in need of one," Jehan said. He could have lied, but if Florent checked with Ignace, then Jehan would most certainly be in trouble. "Putting a dead body into the river isn't a sin."

Florent seemed to consider that for a moment. He then shrugged and said, "Fine. I've done my assignment. I'm going back to the Abbé." With that, Florent strode off into the night.

Reaching into one of his pockets, Jehan removed two coins and then knelt to pick up Absolon's head.

ঙ্ক

Constable Gaubert didn't like what was happening to his town. He had been assigned to the Dordogne region of France soon after the war ended. It was a reward, of a sort, for his service in the military. This part of France was relatively quiet and isolated, so he considered himself a lucky man. His pay was substantial—enough for him to live comfortably, though his work load was rather small.

The people had initially been suspicious of him because he wasn't from the area. He soon gained the trust of the people that mattered, though he couldn't quite see eye to eye with them on every subject. Gaubert never considered himself to be a religious person. Oh, he believed in God, and had prayed to Him many times before battle. But to him, the abbot and the monks were, for lack of a better term, insincere. But he came to an agreement of sorts with Abbot Ignace—a type of truce. The abbot would leave him to do his job and vice versa. So far, it had worked out well.

His initial unpleasant event as constable was at the start of winter when a dead body had been found by some fishermen. People would drown time and again in the river, but this body had no head.

No one was reported missing, and so Gaubert had written it off as the work of brigands further up river. He hadn't given it a second thought until today, several months later.

"There's something unholy happening here," the toothless fisherman said, pointing to his discovery.

Gaubert knelt down by the riverside and inspected the man intertwined in the fisherman's nets—or at least what was left of the man.

"And you say you found him this way?" Gaubert asked. "No sign of his head?"

"With God as my witness, Constable, I found

him as he is."

Closer inspection of the man's neck showed signs that it had been cut off. Gaubert had seen enough death and decapitations during his war service to know that this was no accident. This man's head had been chopped off on purpose.

Gaubert handed the fisherman a few coins. "Keep this quiet until I can investigate further. Also, wrap the body up in blankets and have it taken to the cemetery. I'll let the gravedigger know to expect you."

"As you say, Constable."

This was just the latest in a string of questionable things happening in the town. Abbot Ignace, with his newfound diamond, had caused quite a stir in the area. People were moving in, buying and fixing up old buildings that had been left to rot during the war. With this kind of growth came the good and the bad. The taverns on the edge of town were drawing a more rowdy element into the area, and Gaubert had had to break up more than one brawl. The prison almost always had at least one person being held for this or that. He feared that it would only get worse. With the increase of seedy things happening, Gaubert wondered if this place would one day be known as Sin City.

Chapter 7

"I'm sorry the food is cold, husband." Rosette placed the plate in front of him.

Lucien's father sighed. It was the fourth time this week he had come home late from work, including the last three days in a row. "I don't blame you, Rosette. We were slow today, as often happens on blessing days."

"You were still at the store?" Lucien asked. "I thought tonight you were at the tavern, performing."

Placing a hand over his eyes, Christophe said tiredly, "I had to cancel—I hadn't sold my daily quota in time."

Lucien looked at his mother, who seemed worried.

"Have you tried to explain to Didier that there are fewer customers on blessing days?" Rosette asked.

Christophe stirred the food in front of him, but didn't take a bite. "Didier assures me that more people will be coming along soon enough, though he didn't explain why. He also tells me at least five or six times a day how blessed I am to work for him and if I'm not willing to do what is needed, he could easily replace me."

"Nonsense," Rosette said, her nostrils flaring. "You are the best salesman in town! Well, aside from maybe Ambre, but at least you don't try to seduce your customers to make a sale."

Christophe let out a sad chuckle. "Actually, maybe I should try that."

Lucien knew his father was joking, and assumed his mother did as well. However, the comment still earned his father a strong pinch on the arm from her.

"Let's change the subject, shall we?" Christophe asked. "Remember how the constable was asking around if anyone was missing? Well, it seems Absolon, the tailor, hasn't been seen in days."

"Why was Constable Gaubert asking if someone was missing?" Lucien asked.

"Because a body was found in the river, with its head cut off." His father made a slicing motion across his neck.

"Christophe!" Rosette exclaimed. "Is this one of your stories?"

"No, it's not."

Lucien was glad he had already finished his meal. Talk of such things made him queasy.

"Absolon's wife was able to verify it was his body at the cemetery. Apparently, the constable didn't allow the body to be buried until he was sure no one was missing. Sadly, it turned out that it was someone in town," Christophe continued.

Rosette sat back in her chair and folded her arms. "But wasn't Absolon one of the members of the new religion? Surely the abbot must be embarrassed that one of his congregation—people who are supposed to be blessed and protected—ended up dead in the river."

"Actually, the abbot posted a proclamation just

this very afternoon concerning what happened."

"Oh?"

Christophe nodded. "It said that Absolon had tried to break into the Abbé and steal the diamond divine. The abbot said it had celestial protection from the Lord and anyone who tried to steal the diamond would wind up headless in the river."

"Aren't there monks at the gate to guard the Abbé?" Lucien asked.

"Maybe people are finding another way in. Also, I'm sure the abbot feels anyone who tries to steal it deserves what they get," Rosette interjected. "But we shouldn't talk of such things, husband. You'll give poor Lucien bad dreams."

Christophe nodded wearily. "You're right; I'm sorry." He turned to Lucien. "And you, my son, need to get to bed. It's late."

That night, Lucien had nightmares of headless bodies, writhing in a lake of fire and brimstone, destined to be tormented for eternity.

❧

"I want it and I want it now! I want a blessing today!" came the angry shout from the man at the gate.

Brother Jehan watched on as Brother Florent answered the man through the opened shutter. "What's so important that it can't wait for the abbot to be available?" Florent asked.

"My wife is coming back from a visit to her family in the country. I have just enough gold saved up to pay for a redemption of my sins. I'm afraid my wife will find out what I've been doing while she's been gone." He spoke through gritted teeth.

"If I get a redemption, she can't find fault in my actions because I've been forgiven!"

Jehan took a step closer so he could hear better. "And what sins do you need forgiven?" his fellow monk asked.

"Do I really need to tell them to you?" The man sounded frustrated.

"Yes."

The man sighed. "I've been visiting the taverns on the edge of town. *You* know what I've been doing."

The wiry monk smiled. Jehan was pretty sure what the man was referring to. At the same time, it solidified Jehan's suspicions that Florent knew all too well what the man meant.

Florent looked up at the cloudy heavens. An overcast sky meant that no blessings would be offered that day. Neither rain nor snow had fallen today, for which Jehan was grateful. It had been a long winter—the longest Jehan could recall. The last of the snow had melted the previous day, and he hoped that was a sign spring would finally arrive.

"I'm sorry, but the abbot needs to rest between blessings," Florent said, sounding anything but apologetic. "You'll have to come back another day."

"When? How soon?" the man asked.

Florent responded slowly and deliberately. "Another … day."

With that, the monk closed the shutter.

Christophe couldn't get out of bed. Though the Sabbath was his favorite day of the week, because it was the one day he didn't have to work at the store, he was simply too bone weary to rise.

Though his body didn't move, his thoughts were quite active. It had been a while since his mind was given a chance to think of anything aside from how to sell more items. He missed being able to invent stories, to turn phrases, to sing songs. Songs. Oh, dear, he had promised his wife he would write a song just for her. He loved her; that much couldn't be denied. But what kind of love song could he write that hadn't been written before?

She had many wonderful qualities, things he could write about. But the song also had to have a special meaning just for her. He thought about how well she had raised Lucien. But the love song he wanted to write for her needed to be more personal, more romantic. Perhaps it could be about an event in their lives. Their wedding? That was one option. Or perhaps, it could be about the time they first met.

He reflected on the occasion. It had been at one of the town festivals. There had been a break in the fighting of the war, and people were celebrating. At first, it was thought to be the end of the hostilities, but it didn't last. Rosette's family had just relocated to the area. Their home had been burned down in one of the many battles that had taken place in the northern part of the country.

Christophe always received attention from the girls in town, though none had caught his fancy. For the festival, he had put on his finest outfit, but noticed a small split in one of the seams. His mother sewed it up quickly, but still, he was a bit late to the town square.

There was a full moon in the sky that summer night, and the stars were twinkling brightly. Christophe felt a spring in his step as he heard the music start to play. All the usual people he knew were there, plus some from the surrounding countryside—no doubt looking for a distraction during those difficult times.

He stepped into the crowd and looked over the scene. People tended to clump into small groups—most were young men eyeing the young women, appearing to be gathering enough courage to ask them to dance. Several of the female townspeople his age noticed his arrival, but that wasn't what caught Christophe's attention.

Standing on the far side of the crowd was Rosette. She was surrounded by young men vying for her consideration, each asking her to dance. She was wearing a long, red dress.

Christophe was rooted in place, unable to take his eyes off her. She took notice of him and then did something amazing. She smiled at him.

And it took his breath away.

That was it. That was what he would write his song about. The first time they met. How they danced the night away, cheek to cheek. He remembered how the highlights in her hair caught her eyes. He had never had such a feeling—a feeling of complete and utter love, as he had that night.

Yes, that was to be her song. His song for her—his lady in red.

☙❧

For the first time in several days, the chapel was full. It wasn't lack of desire from the parishioners that kept them away, or that the abbot was actually ill, rather it was a raging storm. But finally, the clouds parted and the sun shone once again, allowing Ignace to hold services.

So far, no one had seemed to make the connection that the blessings took place only on sunny days, but Ignace felt he had better address it before rumors started to spread. He stood at the altar mid and looked down at the anxious faces.

"My dear people," Ignace said in introduction, "it's truly wonderful to have you here. Before we proceed to the blessings, there are two things I must tell you."

He waited a moment to allow all of their eyes to be focused on him. "First of all, let me address the disturbing news of Absolon. Yes, Absolon was a member of this blessed congregation. And yet, he made two serious mistakes. First, he would intentionally sin with the aim of being forgiven at a later time. However, he died before he could receive that blessing, and will spend eternity in Hell being punished for his actions."

Ignace noticed several people shudder at the thought—a good sign indeed. "I would strongly encourage all of you to make donations for pre-forgiveness. I know the sacrifice is greater for such a blessing, but the thought of any of you suffering the same fate as Absolon weighs heavy on my heart.

"And as for his second mistake, I will discuss this point more in a moment." The abbot paused, allowing a small smile to show on his face. "On a more positive note, I wish to tell you of a beautiful dream I had recently. I dreamt of a man walking up a rocky road. He was searching for a place where there was a sacred stone. On this stone was the word of the Lord. And from the top of the mountain he brought it back to his people. The lightning struck and the thunder roared as he lifted it up in the name of the Lord. There, many waited for the new revelation—one that came from the Lord through Moses.

"However, Moses was a flawed man. He was not great of speech. In fact, Aaron was used as his mouthpiece. The people accepted this, and through their faith, they were blessed."

The abbot took in a deep breath and then sighed dramatically. "I, too, am flawed," Ignace announced.

There was a gasp from the congregation, followed by nervous whispers. Never had he, as the abbot, made such a statement. Ignace took a moment, then held up both hands for everyone to quiet down.

"Just as with Moses, the Lord has given me a physical challenge to keep me humble. Unlike Moses, I am able to speak for myself. However, my physical body is greatly affected by the weather. When there are clouds in the sky, my joints ache so badly that I do not have the strength to climb the stairs to the altar high. I have pleaded with the Lord to have this burden lifted from me, but in His wisdom, He allows it to remain.

"I've even gone so far as to ask that one of the monks be allowed to perform the blessings when I am unable to do so, but once again, the Lord has told me that I alone am assigned this duty. Only I am blessed with the ability to use the diamond divine. Anyone else who tries will most certainly be struck down by the Lord. This was Absolon's second mistake I mentioned earlier. I believe he was planning to steal the diamond divine, and that is why Absolon ended up in the river without his head. Why would he try to take it? Perhaps to get the blessings without making the needed sacrifices. Also, how he lost his head and was put in the river is one of the mysteries of the Lord. You, as the common man, are not meant to know. But it is proof that the Lord will not allow any unhallowed hand to desecrate this sacred object. I beseech you, do not attempt to approach the stone. I would that no one else suffers the punishment Absolon is receiving in Hell."

He noticed several people's faces had turned quite pale—perhaps they had considered taking the diamond for themselves? Well, after what he had told them, the abbot doubted they would give it any more serious thought.

Then Ignace showed the people his warmest smile. "We are in the Lord's favor today as the sun is shining brightly. While we have time, we will proceed with the blessings."

He turned to the elder monk standing off to the side of the altars. "Brother Maximilien, please read the name of the first person to be blessed today."

ଓଃ

"I brought you some bread and cheese, Father," Lucien said, holding out the tied cloth sack

his mother had asked him to deliver.

Christophe smiled. "Thank you, son."

Lucien looked around the store. It was lunch time in the middle of the week, so there weren't any customers. "Do you mind if I stay here a bit while you eat?" Lucien asked.

"Do I mind? I would be delighted! Didier is taking advantage of the nice spring day to go on one of his hunting trips. We won't be bothered by him."

With that, Christophe opened the sack and divided out the bread and cheese between him and Lucien.

"What's he hunting today?"

Christophe sighed. "Anything that moves. While other townspeople hunt to put meat on their tables, or to sell the pelts of animals, Didier hunts for the sake of hunting. I've never seen him return with anything, though he often tells me the stories of his triumphs."

"So … he just leaves whatever he kills where it falls?"

"He must, if he actually kills anything at all."

The door opened and in walked one of the town's woodworkers. Fabrice was a large man with rough hands, but a smooth smile. Lucien had met the man a few times before when he had stopped by to visit his father at work.

"Good day to you, Christophe," Fabrice said.

"And to you, my friend."

"Oh! And here is your son, Lucien. It's good to see you again, boy." Fabrice offered his hand, which Lucien took and shook as firmly as he could.

"Nice grip you have there," Fabrice said.

"Thank you, sir," Lucien responded.

The two men then started talking business. Fabrice needed supplies for his shop, plus he wanted to know what the store was running low on so that he could fill the order. Lucien had always been fascinated with taking something as ordinary as a tree and turning it into the marvelous items Fabrice created.

"So, Lucien," Fabrice said after concluding his transactions, "I understand you turned thirteen recently. Have you given any thought to what you will do when you become a man?"

The question caught him a bit off guard. His father had always taught him to be honest, but in a way not to offend. "Up until recently, I always assumed I would be conscripted as a soldier. But now that the war is over, I'm not sure."

"The war appears to be over," Fabrice said. "With power-hungry men in the land, I'm sure there will be more battles in the future. Sometimes I feel like they are little boys, just spoiling for a fight. I will never know how men can see the wisdom in a war."

Lucien frowned. "Do you honestly think there would be another war after all that was lost in the last one?"

"Well, what would you do if you knew the leaders of the area were about to go to war, eh, Lucien?"

He chewed on his lower lip for a moment before responding,

"I'd say we stick them in a room together and make *them* fight it out—until they see nothing from nothing will leave nothing at all."

Fabrice's eyebrows shot up. "Very poetic. You sound like your father. Maybe you're destined to become a bard"

Lucien noticed his father's countenance fall a bit at the suggestion. It had been several months since his father had been able to perform at the tavern. But as quickly as it had come, his father's expression changed again.

"Perhaps you could take Lucien on as an apprentice," Christophe offered. "You never had a son of your own."

Fabrice nodded. "Wasn't from lack of trying. But after we had our fourth daughter, I gave up any notions that I'd have a son. And yes, I think he would make a good apprentice. What do you think, Lucien?"

The sudden offer that would impact the rest of his life was intimidating, to say the least. "May I talk it over with my mother and father?"

"Certainly," Fabrice said. "This isn't a decision to be taken lightly. I've been thinking about bringing on an apprentice, and though you aren't quite of age, I believe you would do well."

Lucien couldn't wait to tell Guy and Henri about the chance to become Fabrice's apprentice. The more he thought about it, the more interesting it sounded. His father suggested watching Fabrice work for a few days before he made a decision, which was sound advice.

He looked for Guy and Henri in their usual haunts. However, with the days getting warmer and longer, they could have been any of a number of places. With the sun starting to set, he decided to stop by Henri's house.

Dusk meant dinner time, and even though Henri would leave his house after dinner most nights, he always went home for the evening meal.

Henri lived in the wealthier part of town. His house was two stories high, with large windows in the front and a proper metal fence. Whether by luck or fate, Henri and Guy were approaching the house at the same time, from a different direction.

"Hello!" Henri called out.

"Hello!" Guy echoed.

Lucien waved a hand in greeting. When they were close enough, Lucien said, "I've been looking for you two. Where have you been?"

"We've been on a scouting mission." Henri grinned. Guy blushed at the statement.

"Oh? Scouting what?"

Henri motioned with his head in the direction they had come. "Surely you've heard of the new taverns on the edge of town, and what goes on there."

He now understood why Guy had blushed. "Let me guess, you are trying to find a way to either sneak in or get a good look through one of the windows."

Smacking Guy on the arm, Henri said, "See, I told you Lucien was a smart one." Then facing him, Henri asked, "We could use your help. Will you come with us after dinner? Guy is staying; you might as well."

"Ah, thanks, but my parents will wonder where I am if I don't make it home soon," Lucien said as an excuse. "But I did have some news to tell you."

He went on to explain about his chance of becoming an apprentice. While Guy seemed impressed by the idea, Henri appeared indifferent.

"Well, I guess you'll have to start making money at some point in time," Henri said, "and I hear Fabrice does very well for himself. In fact, I heard—wait, what's that?"

Henri was pointing to smoke coming from behind his neighbor's house, just barely visible in the day's fading light. The smell of smoke wasn't uncommon in town, as people used fires to cook their meals, but to see smoke coming from a place other than a chimney in this part of town was odd.

"Let's go take a look!" Henri said.

The three boys went in the front gate of Henri's house and then skirted around to the back to investigate. Henri motioned for them to be quiet as they approached and hid behind some bushes.

There was a large fire built behind the neighboring house. A couple of servants were throwing various items into the fire, mostly pieces of parchment and the like. It didn't make any sense to Lucien. Why build such a big fire to burn pieces of paper that could have easily been burned in an indoor fireplace?

"Renaud and Jocelyne live next door," Henri whispered. "He's rather unpleasant—he owns many vineyards in the hills. He's often gone to inspect them. Jocelyne, on the other hand, is very pleasant and absolutely stunning. Ever since I was young I've been trying to catch glimpses of her."

"So what do you think is going on?" Lucien asked, keeping his voice low as well.

"No idea," Henri replied.

Guy spoke up. "My father has been over to their house a lot the last few weeks. He said he's been commissioned to do a painting of Jocelyne. He usually does a bunch of sketches first, on parchments like they are burning in the fire."

"That still doesn't explain why—" Lucien started to say until one of the servants came out holding a large painting. From the light of the fire, Lucien could see that it was a portrait of a lady. And she wasn't wearing any clothes.

The servant threw the painting on top of the fire, but it slid down to one side and didn't catch fire right away. Before Lucien could say anything, Henri bolted toward the fire.

The servants had gone back inside and seemed not to hear or see Henri dashing toward the flames. Lucien's friend arrived at the painting and grabbed it by the top of the frame, even though the bottom was quite on fire by now. Henri pulled the work of art away and tossed it to the ground, then stomped on the part that was on fire until it was put out. He quickly retreated back to where his friends were waiting for him behind the shrubs.

Henri proudly held up the painting, or at least what was left of it, in front of him and Guy. Everything from the mid-shoulder and down had burned away, leaving only her face and upper torso.

"Are you crazy?" Lucien asked. "What if they had spotted you? They were burning it for a reason!"

Henri looked startled. "Do you think I could let such a chance pass me by? I only wish I had gotten there earlier so I could have saved more of it." Henri turned the painting around and smiled. "Although, this isn't too bad."

"I think I better go home before my parents get

worried," Lucien declared.

Henri acknowledged Lucien's statement only by waving one hand in his direction while he and Guy continued to stare at the painting.

ଔଓ

Ambre placed her offering on the altar low in front of Jehan. She then faced and smiled at him suggestively. "This offering frees me of any sins I may commit for the next week," she said, just loud enough that Jehan could hear. "Certainly as a monk, you are allowed the same privileges."

Her meaning was clear. And it wasn't that Jehan hadn't given the subject the same thought. However, despite all that Jehan had seen, somewhere deep inside, he doubted the power of the diamond. Of course, he hadn't shared this with anyone. Surely he would be cast out of the Abbé if it was discovered that he, one of the abbot's men, lacked the faith Ignace demanded. Actually, that was it. Jehan realized it wasn't the diamond that was in question here; it was his own faith. And until he had enough faith, he wouldn't be able to fully receive the blessings from the famous gem. As well, he had never been offered nor had he asked for a blessing.

"Alas, Ambre, I have been assigned a great number of responsibilities for the upcoming week," Jehan said in a low voice.

"A pity," she purred. "Perhaps one day you will be free enough from your responsibilities. In the meantime, at least come visit me in the market or gardens when you can."

She brushed up against him as she walked by to get in line for her blessing. That brief touch sent a thrill through Jehan's body. Yes. He must certainly develop faith in the diamond, and soon.

Chapter 8

"Ah! Well met!" Christophe said to the young couple that entered the store. "Welcome to La boutique de désirs. My name is Christophe. How may I help you today?"

He noticed that they were holding hands, something he and his wife had done when they were first married. When was the last time he had taken her somewhere to give him the chance to hold her hand?

"It's nice to meet you, Christophe. I'm Luc, and this is my wife Cecile."

Christophe came out from behind the counter and offered his hand in greeting. "I don't believe we've met before. Are you new to our town?"

Luc took Christophe's hand in a firm shake. "We're new, yes. It seems we're not the only newcomers to town, either."

"Ah, yes, we've seen quite a few new people move into the area."

"It's because of the diamond divine, isn't it?" Cecile asked. Christophe noted that her voice was rather pleasant. He also noted something else about Cecile: her eyes seemed to be looking not at him, but through him.

"Oh, so you've heard of the miracle that the Abbé St. Pierre received, have you?" Christophe said, trying not to look at Cecile.

Luc nodded. "Word has traveled, yes. Have you seen it?"

"I've seen it, yes," Christophe said carefully. He didn't want his customers to find out he wasn't a member of the congregation. "But tell me, what do you do for a living?"

If Luc was put off by the sudden change in subject, he didn't let it show. "I'm a craftsman by trade. We just moved into a house that was recently owned by, oh, what was his name, sweetheart?"

"Absolon," Cecile responded. "A tailor."

Christophe had heard that Absolon's wife had fled after her husband was killed and branded as a thief.

"Though his workshop was set up for a tailor, I can make adjustments to do my work," Luc said.

"If I recall correctly, he lived in a nice house. You must be doing well in your craft to afford such a place," Christophe said. Hopefully this couple had come here to spend enough to meet his daily quota.

"Actually, we got it for a song," Cecile said. "We didn't dare ask why. Luc inspected the house inside and out before we agreed to buy it, and it was in immaculate condition."

"Well, sometimes God blesses us in ways we don't understand at the time," Luc said. "Speaking of which, how do we go about seeing this diamond divine?"

Christophe felt his shoulders tense up a bit. But he then put on his best smile and said, "Simply go to the gate at the Abbé St. Pierre and ask one of the monks. They'll instruct you on what is needed."

"We shall do so," Luc said. "Thank you."

"But I'm sure you came in here for more than

just directions," Christophe said. He opened his arms wide. "We have the finest selection of wares in the area. What were you looking to buy?"

"My wife doesn't see well," Luc said, patting his wife's hand. "That's one reason we came—to get a blessing to restore her eyesight. In the meantime, we need more candlesticks. The brighter it is, the easier it is for her to see."

"Ah, let me show you what we have. In fact, we just got some in a recent shipment—they are of a very fine quality," Christophe said. He started to head to the shelf where they were kept.

"Actually," Luc said, "as I stated before, I'm a crafter and could make my own, though I specialize in larger items. We just need some simple ones to get us by until I can make some."

Christophe felt the sale starting to slip away from him. "I can understand that. However, keep in mind that you will most likely start to receive visitors and potential customers soon. You'll want to make a strong impression from the start in order to win their business. I've seen where people in this town make decisions off of first impressions."

The young crafter looked at his wife. "What do you think, sweetheart?"

"He makes a point, and he knows this area better than we do."

Luc turned back to Christophe. "All right then, show us what you recommend."

Christophe took them over to a set of eight silver candlesticks. "These are the finest we have. Their design is unique, as they were brought in from Spain. They'll certainly impress any who see them."

The crafter picked one up and looked at it with

a practiced eye. "This is amazing workmanship. I've seen a few other items from Spain, and I notice some similarities in the style. It seems the Spanish train their crafters in certain techniques."

"As you can see, we only have eight in stock, so they must be sold in either a set of four or all eight. Though I recommend you take all eight so you'll be the only ones with candlesticks like these. So, which will it be? Four or eight?"

He noticed the younger man frown at the price listed. Cecile's brow furrowed a bit as well. Christophe fought the urge to say anything. This was the part in a sale where the first person to speak "loses," as Didier would call it.

"These are quite a bit more than we had planned on spending," Luc said.

Again, Christophe said nothing.

"But he makes a good point, Luc," Cecile said. "If you want to establish your business here, we need to bring in and keep customers."

Luc frowned, then blew out a deep breath. "I guess we better take all eight of these then."

"Excellent choice," Christophe said. "Now, let me show you the fine tablecloths we have to go with these."

By the time Luc and Cecile left, Christophe had sold them eight candlesticks, three tablecloths and a set of dishes. He tried not to flinch when he noticed that he had taken all but three of Luc's coins from his pouch.

He hit his quota for the day—a rarity to be done before lunch. He really wished that anything else he sold would count for the following day.

Only once had he sold enough to earn the

bonus he'd been promised, and even then, Didier had been reluctant to give it to him.

The afternoon passed by fairly quietly, which allowed Christophe to let his mind work on the love song he was writing for Rosette. He had several lines written and had come up with a basic melody he liked. Sadly, most days were so filled with the stress of hitting his sales expectation that by the time he got home, he was simply too tired.

It was only on the Sabbath evening, the time when he had been away from work the longest, that he felt his muse stir. But then, he also wanted to spend time with his wife and son—often he wouldn't spend any time working on the song.

But it would all be worth it someday. He would be able to afford the blessing of health on his wife. Perhaps then he could find other work; the town was growing enough that he might be able to find a less demanding boss. And with other work, he could go back to playing in the taverns and focus on what he truly enjoyed.

His ruminations were interrupted when Didier strode into the store, looking as full of himself as ever. In his hand he held a long metal pole with a cloth of some type wrapped around the end.

"Christophe! Where are all the customers?" Didier demanded.

"We had some earlier. In fact, I sold—"

The owner of La boutique de désirs interrupted Christophe's comment before he could finish. "I was expecting you to at least be helping someone. But it looks like I'll have to do your job and bring in more customers."

He motioned to the item he was holding. "And

this is just the thing to do so."

"What is it?"

Didier put the bottom of the pole on the ground and then carefully unraveled the banner attached to the other end. It was made from a purple cloth with a silver border. In the center was an embroidered diamond that looked very much like the diamond divine.

"The abbot allowed us to buy these standards to hang in front of our shops," Didier said proudly. "He had another vision. Merchants would be blessed by displaying that we are part of the Lord's chosen. These banners are how we are to distinguish that we are above the rest of the merchants moving into town."

Christophe examined the banner carefully. It was simply stunning, and must have been expensive.

"Carefully hang this banner above our sign so that everyone can see it," Didier instructed. "The donation I made for this was certainly a sacrifice."

"How much was it?"

Didier looked offended. "It's not proper to ask such things. Just know that it will be worth it. You'll see. And as a demonstration of my faith, and to recoup what I donated, you are going to have to sell an additional ten coins' worth of items per day."

"An additional..." Christophe started to say. He was barely making his quota now, and even then, he had to convince people of their needs instead of listening to their needs and matching what would be best for them.

"With this," Didier said, holding the banner up, "you'll be able to sell that much more easily!"

ଓଃଃ

Guy looked out of breath, which often happened when he ran a distance of any length. His face was red from overexertion, but more than that, he appeared distraught.

"Lucien, you must come with me, quickly!"

It was mid-afternoon and Lucien had been in Fabrice's shop all day. He hadn't committed fully to being the man's apprentice, but he had agreed to spend a few days observing.

"What's the hurry then, lad?" Fabrice asked. "Is something the matter?"

Guy nodded, still trying to catch his breath.

"What happened?" Lucien asked. This time, Guy shook his head. "No, not here. Just come with me, please!"

Fabrice put a hand on Lucien's shoulder. "Go ahead, we can finish up tomorrow."

After thanking his potential mentor, Lucien removed the heavy leather apron he had been lent and walked outside with Guy.

"All right, now tell me what is going on."

Guy had stopped panting, but was now starting to blubber like a baby. "It's my father! He's been accused of murder."

"What? How? When?"

Lucien's round friend took in a deep breath, then let it out in stages as he continued to cry. "Just come with me. The constable is at my house now. I need you to be a witness that my father is innocent."

"All right, let's go. You can tell me the details on the way."

"No, I can't. It's too gruesome. You'll have to hear it from the constable."

They traveled quickly to Guy's house. When they entered they saw Claude, Guy's father, sitting on a chair with his head buried in his hands. Constable Gaubert was talking to another man Lucien recognized, but didn't know by name.

"Father! I've brought Lucien. He can prove you didn't do it!" Guy proclaimed.

This caught the constable's attention. He stopped talking to the other man and approached Lucien.

"Lucien, is it?" the constable asked, reaching out to offer his hand.

"Yes, sir," Lucien responded, shaking the man's hand.

"Please sit down; I need to hear your side of the story."

"*His* side of the story?" the other man asked, anger evident in his voice.

Gaubert turned to the man and said, "Yes, Renaud, there are at least two sides to every story. Now be quiet as I talk to Lucien here."

Lucien remembered that he had seen Renaud often visiting the Abbé St. Pierre—and if he was the man Lucien thought he was, Renaud had been born into wealth and lived in one of the nicest houses in the area. In fact, he realized that he lived next to Henri.

Both the constable and Lucien sat down on a plush couch in the sitting room. "Now, tell me what you know," Gaubert asked.

"I'm not sure what this is about," Lucien said.

"Guy didn't tell you?"

Lucien shook his head.

"Jocelyne, Renaud's wife, was found hanging from a wall in their house. By the looks of it, she'd been there for several days—I'd say, almost a week."

The thought of something so gruesome made Lucien feel sick to his stomach. He took in a deep breath and then asked, "But how does this involve Guy's father?"

"Renaud claims that Jocelyne begged him to let Claude into their house to paint a portrait of her," Gaubert said.

"Let me tell it," Renaud said. He stomped over to where they were sitting. The constable was about to say something, but Renaud started speaking first.

"At first, everything was fine. But after a while he was driving me mad. Sitting there day after day, with my wife in the palm of his hand. It was 'Madam please do this and madam please do that.' You've never heard such display. But Claude didn't mind—he was taking his time, and it was me that had to pay!"

"I don't understand," Lucien said. "You're saying he killed her instead of painting a portrait of her? Why would he do such a thing?"

Renaud's face turned red. "You've not heard it all! He said he needed to study her before he could create the work of art. One day, he said, 'Madam, I think we should take a walk in the woods. You understand, it's the light.' At that point in time, did I mind? No, I was so kind when they came back in the middle of the night. Over time, she only had eyes for him and his lies, and for me? Not a glance! Not a single one! There was a period of time when I had to leave to see about my family's vineyards, and when I came back, I found her hanging on the wall. You see, he had made a work of art using her, just not the way she intended." Renaud pointed to Claude. "It's that painter! It's him! He's to blame!"

This didn't make any sense to Lucien. Yes, Guy's father was a bit of a charmer; he'd always been that way with the ladies. Guy's mother had died when he was young, so Lucien didn't think anything of it when Claude was seen with other women. But why would he kill one of them?

"So what makes you think I can say anything to prove he didn't do it?" Lucien asked.

The constable looked deep into his eyes. "Tell me what you took from behind Renaud's house."

Lucien tensed up. No wonder Guy hadn't told him what this was about. Surely when his mother and father found out, he would be in trouble. At the same time, having his parents upset at him wasn't nearly as bad as being blamed for murder.

"*I* never took anything from his yard," Lucien said, trying to see if there was a way out of this without getting in trouble.

The constable folded his arms and lowered his eyebrows. "Lucien, you were there when someone took something, and I think you know exactly what I'm talking about."

There was no way out of this. Lucien decided he should just tell the truth. He told how he, Guy and Henri had seen something burning behind Renaud's house.

"And what was being burned?"

"A painting."

"Lies!" Renaud shouted. "He's obviously trying

to cover for his friend. Claude never created a painting!"

Pointing a thick finger at Renaud, Gaubert said, "Be quiet, or I shall lock you up for interfering with an investigation."

"You wouldn't dare! *My* wife was killed!"

The constable began to stand, which quickly shut up Renaud. Focusing his attention back on Lucien, he asked, "What was on the painting?"

"A woman, though it was mostly burned. Only the shoulders and up were left."

"So why are you afraid to tell me about this painting?"

Lucien put a hand over his eyes. "Because before the painting caught fire, we saw that the lady was naked, even though most of it burned before Henri could save it. If my parents knew what I'd seen, I'd be in so much trouble."

"I understand. Listen carefully to me; this next part is important. Where is that painting now?" Gaubert asked.

"Henri took it. Speaking of which, where is Henri? Shouldn't he be here as well?"

"I couldn't find him," Guy said. "And I knew where to find you. But I know he still has it. We were looking at it just last night."

The constable stood up and faced Renaud. "So, Renaud, you said there was no painting actually produced. But Claude claims he finished it and hadn't seen Jocelyne while you were gone.

"When we find this painting, is it going to be of your wife like Claude claims it to be?"

"And so what if it is?" Renaud asked, starting to look smug.

"It makes more sense to me that you saw the painting, and in a jealous rage killed your wife and hung her on the wall to make it look as if Claude had done it. You then took the painting and tried to burn it, but these boys took it before it burned completely. How am I doing so far?"

Renaud's response was to grin—in a way that looked a bit crazed to Lucien—and then he said, "We need to go to the Abbé St. Pierre and talk to the abbot before I say anything else on this matter."

Chapter 9

It was a cloudy day. Ignace used to dread cloudy days, but he now enjoyed them. It meant no blessings would have to be performed. Granted, his joints ached a bit when it was overcast, he had told the people as much, but as long as he relaxed, he was fine. He sat in his new chair—one designed just for him, with deep cushions and gilded edges. The only thing better than admiring the chair from afar was sitting in it. From here, he could also admire himself in his mirror. He looked magnificent.

Bastien had been bringing him bowls of food throughout the day, and in between naps, he had plenty to eat. Yes, it had been a perfect day. That was until Brother Jehan came and disturbed him.

"Please forgive the intrusion, Abbot. But the constable is here and is quite insistent that he see you," the large monk said.

"What's it about?" Ignace asked. He popped another cherry tomato into his mouth.

Jehan cleared his throat. "He says it's about a murder."

The abbot ate another of the small tomatoes, waited to swallow it, and then said, "Murders are the business of the constable. I won't be doing his work for him."

"But Abbot Ignace, what if he is here about Absolon's murder?"

Ignace's hand froze above the bowl of food. "What did you say?"

Jehan hesitated before he spoke again. "What if he is here about Absolon?"

"That's better. Absolon wasn't murdered. The Lord took his life. So, as I said, tell the constable he must do his own work," Ignace said. He waved Jehan away, but the monk didn't move.

"Please forgive me, Abbot Ignace; I tried to tell him to go away when he first arrived, but he wouldn't go. I even closed the shutter on him, but he continued to pound on it until I opened it again. At that point he said he would enter the Abbé by force if you would not see him."

Ignace felt anger start to build inside him. *How dare the constable make such demands!* It took some effort, but Ignace got up from his chair.

"Bring him to the courtyard, and tell him I'll be there shortly," Ignace said through gritted teeth.

"Yes, Abbot."

"And Brother Jehan, your primary responsibility here at the monastery is to keep unwanted people out. The Lord is displeased that you have failed Him today."

The monk looked as if he were about to say something, but then simply bowed his head. "Understood, Abbot. I will do better from here on out." With that, Jehan left.

Ignace straightened his robes and then let out a large sigh. *It's a shame I have to deal with such unpleasantries at the end of a perfect day.*

Gaubert stood with his arms folded and tapped his foot impatiently. "You did say the abbot was on his way, correct?"

The large monk in front of him nodded. Flanking Gaubert were Renaud and Claude. He had insisted that the painter accompany them to the Abbé to hear what Renaud had to say. It seemed no amount of threatening intimidated Renaud, and the man refused to say anything more than he would speak only in front of the abbot.

Finally, a door opened on the other side of the courtyard. Abbot Ignace toddled out, seeming to be in no hurry to arrive to the men who waited for him. When he got close enough, Gaubert said, "My apologies for disturbing you, Abbot."

"I would think threatening to force your way into this holy place would demand more than a simple apology, but we will discuss that later," Ignace said. "What do you want?"

"There's been a murder," Gaubert said.

Gaubert thought Brother Jehan tense up when he mentioned the murder. But his full attention was on the abbot, not the monk, so he couldn't be sure.

"And who was murdered?" Ignace asked.

"Jocelyne, the wife of Renaud, both members of your congregation."

This time Gaubert did watch for Jehan's response, and he noticed the monk became visibly more relaxed. It was something he'd have to investigate later.

"Constable Gaubert," Ignace said forcefully, "murders are your business. Not mine. Just because they are true followers does not give you the right to bother me and threaten the monks here."

Gaubert didn't let the statement rile him. In a calm voice, he replied, "Oh, it wasn't me who was insistent upon seeing you."

The abbot frowned. "Then who?"

"It was me, Abbot Ignace." Renaud stepped forward.

"Renaud?" the abbot said, clearly surprised. "You have been one of the most faithful and generous members of the Lord's church. Why would you make such a demand?"

Gaubert fully expected Renaud to accuse Claude of the murder of his wife, which was why the painter was here as well. Through all of this, Claude had remained very quiet except to keep stating that he had not killed Jocelyne. What Renaud said took him by surprise.

"I killed my wife in a crime of passion and blamed it on Claude." Renaud pointed to the painter.

"Why didn't you just admit this earlier?" Gaubert demanded. "You could have saved us all a lot of trouble!"

"As well as keeping the abbot from being disturbed," Jehan said.

Renaud smiled. "Don't you see? I'm blameless before the Lord."

"Blameless?" Gaubert was bewildered. Certainly this man was mad. "You just admitted to killing your wife and trying to place the responsibility on someone else, and now you claim innocence?"

"When was this, Renaud?" Ignace asked.

"It was the day after the Sabbath," Renaud said, sounding more confident each time he spoke.

Ignace appeared deep in thought for a moment. He then turned to Gaubert and said, "Renaud is correct. He is blameless before the Lord."

"What?" Gaubert said, balling his fists. "How can you say that?"

The abbot turned his nose up slightly when he responded. "Renaud made a rather large donation on the Sabbath. The blessing he requested was one of absolution for a week's time. Therefore, any transgressions he committed this week were pre-forgiven."

"Pre-forgiven? Are you serious? Renaud admits he hung his wife on a wall like some deranged piece of art and then tried to have another man arrested, and you tell me that the Lord permits such things?"

Ignace stared at Gaubert, a look of pure hatred on his face. "How dare you speak blasphemy in this holy place! You are not one of the Lord's chosen, so I don't expect you to understand."

Gaubert had heard enough. "All right. Renaud may be blameless before this Lord of yours, but he is not blameless in the eyes of the law. I'm arresting him and he will hang for his crime. Once he reaches St. Peter's Gate, they can sort it out there."

"Sanctuary!" Renaud cried out. "Sanctuary! I seek sanctuary from this heathen!"

"Granted," Ignace said magnanimously.

Renaud smirked at Gaubert.

"Now, Brother Jehan," the abbot said, "escort these other men from the Abbé."

© ⸙ ©

Christophe stumbled as he entered his house. His loss of balance wasn't due to partaking of the strong drink, but rather, from being physically and mentally exhausted. Didier had been correct—the hanging of the banner had brought in more customers, but the type of customers that came now were much more demanding and wanted to be waited on hand and foot. He was meeting his new quota, but just barely, and even then it wasn't reaching the sales number that was the challenge—it was keeping the customers happy.

Rosette was sitting and waiting for him, as she did every night. Except tonight, she was dressed up nicer than normal. It made him wonder if he had forgotten something important. It would have been easy to do; his mind was too full of the events from work for him to really focus on anything else.

"Hello, dear husband." She smiled and stood.

"Rosette," Christophe said. "You look beautiful. You look wonderful. You're like an angel heaven sent to me."

She gave him a knowing look. "You see that I'm dressed up and think you've forgotten something, so you try to flatter me with that silver tongue of yours?"

Christophe gave her a tired smile in return. "Did it work? And what did I forget?"

"Come." She walked to a padded bench they had near the window. "Let's talk for a moment."

Even though he was hungry and tired, he couldn't refuse his wife's request. Once they had both sat down, Christophe told his wife, "I'm so sorry for whatever I forgot. Please, tell me what I can do to make it better."

She placed her hand on his cheek and gently said, "Dear, there are only two things I've ever wanted from you: love and time. When we were first married, we were so happy. We traveled from place to place, making money from your performances. During those times of war, people appreciated the distraction. I even supported your decision to work for Didier after Lucien was born, though I would have rather you continued with your storytelling."

"Are you telling me you aren't happy now?" Christophe started to feel a bit defensive.

"Darling, I am happy. I have a wonderful family. I just want to see my husband more often. You've been spending so much time at work—"

Christophe stood, feeling angry. "Rosette, I'm doing this for you! I figured it out. If I can keep up my sales until just before winter, I'll be able to afford to join the congregation at the Abbé St. Pierre. And with that, I can get you a blessing of health before winter comes."

She simply looked at him warmly, then patted the seat next to her. Christophe knew he was being overly sensitive—who wouldn't be if they were as tired as he was? He took in several deep breaths and then sat back down.

"I'm sorry," he said quietly. "I'm just so tired, and—"

Rosette put a finger to his lips. "Darling, I appreciate your concern for me. Yes, each winter is harder on me. Will the diamond be able to prevent me from getting sick? I have my doubts, but I know that you believe it will. If I am to die this winter—"

"Please don't say that." Christophe felt tears coming to his eyes. "Please."

She took his hands in hers. "If I am to die this

winter, I would much rather spend my last days having you by my side more. Quit working for Didier. I'm sure you can find work at the taverns singing your songs and telling your tales."

"Rosette, please, I have to try this. I'm so close. Even if there is a *chance* that it will work, if I can show enough faith, I have to try. I can't sit by and watch you wither away when there is something I can do about it."

For a long moment, his wife looked searchingly into his eyes. "All right, husband. Make me this promise, however. After I've received this blessing, you'll quit working for Didier."

Christophe felt relief. He could do this. He could get her this blessing and then quit. He could endure.

"Yes, Rosette, I promise."

He could tell she believed him. Her eyes sparkled and the corners of her mouth curved up. "You must be hungry," she said. "How about I be the storyteller tonight while you eat?"

Oh, how he loved this woman. "I'd like that," he said.

In short order, he was at the table with his meal in front of him. She sat down next to him and placed her hand on her chin. "Let's see now…a story."

He was curious what she would tell him. She'd always been practical, and while she told him she enjoyed listening to his stories, she never showed any interest in inventing her own.

"I know." She sat up, straightening her back. "This story takes place several years ago, in an area not far from here."

He tried to ask something, but she hushed him and motioned for him to keep eating. "It was a beautiful spring day. The setting was a country churchyard. Turtledoves were perched in the steeple and singing a wonderful tune. There were flowers in the graveyard next to the church with bees buzzing to and fro."

It was Christophe's turn to smile. He knew the exact place.

"On a hill overlooking the churchyard, where the river met the mill, a lovely girl was coming down to give her hand to the man she loved. You see, it was her wedding day. She was dressed in simple white with flowers in her hair. There were musicians close by playing a wedding march as she approached the altar. Around the churchyard were the preacher and his people, as well as the handsome groom. The preacher greeted her and asked, 'Will you take this man to be your wedded husband? To honor and love in the eyes of God above?' She of course answered yes."

Christophe had stopped eating. His eyes filled with tears as he recalled their wedding day. They had decided to have the ceremony performed where Rosette had grown up. The war had shifted to the east, so they were clear to have the ceremony there. It seemed so long ago, yet the images remained vivid in his mind. Life had seemed so full of promise then. He understood what she was doing. His dear, sweet wife was reminding him of hope and the promise of a better future.

"Do you remember what the preacher said that day, my dear husband?" she asked. She seemed to know full well that he did.

"Yes," Christophe replied. "He said to let our love shine on."

Again, she placed her hand on his cheek. "That's want I want. I want our love to shine on. I want it to be brighter than the sun. We need to live for every moment, before that moment is gone."

He promised himself he would be a better husband. He would. But first, he needed to get Rosette the blessing of health. Without it, he feared she wouldn't survive the upcoming winter.

ଓ෴ဢ

The blessings were nearly done for the day, and Jehan couldn't be happier. His responsibility was to guide the people from the alter low, where they made their donations, to where they needed to stand to receive their blessing. By now, those getting blessed knew the routine so there was little Jehan had to actually do aside from keeping things moving along.

However, the next people in line were new to the church. If he recalled correctly, they were Luc and Cecile—a young married couple that just moved to the area.

The man set his donation on the alter low—it was an amount of gold that Jehan hadn't seen donated before. Surely as new members, they had made a mistake.

"Luc, is it?" Jehan asked.

"Yes, I'm Luc."

Jehan tilted his head toward the donation. "And what blessing were you donating for?"

"It's one of health, for my wife, Cecile. Her eyesight is failing."

That's why the amount donated was unfamiliar to Jehan—no one had asked for a blessing of health before. Forgiveness of sins or promise of eternal life didn't have visible changes to the person, except for their expressions or the way they carried themselves after the blessing. If Jehan had any doubts about the power of the diamond, this request for a blessing of health amplified them. What if it didn't work? Would it show the people the diamond didn't really have the power the abbot claimed?

"Ah, I see. One moment. Please remain here," Jehan said.

The large monk then waited for the man who had just been blessed to walk away before he approached the alter high. Once there, he took a few steps up so he could talk to the abbot without being overheard.

"Abbot Ignace," Jehan whispered, "the next blessing is a request for health."

"So? Bring them forward."

"But, Abbot, the blessing is a request to fix her eyesight," Jehan said.

For a moment, the abbot didn't say anything—he simply stared down at the monk. "And what is your concern with this, Brother Jehan?"

"What if it doesn't work?"

Jehan noticed the abbot's ears start to turn red—not a good sign. "Brother Jehan, I'm very disappointed in you. Bring forth the young woman and watch."

The monk went back down the steps and then took Cecile by the arm. "Please, come with me," Jehan said.

After escorting her to the place where the

blessings were given, Jehan took a step back.

"My beloved people," the abbot said loudly, "you are about to witness history. For the first time, a blessing of health has been requested. And what is your name, my dear?"

"Cecile."

"And tell us, what ails you?" Ignace asked, once again loud enough for everyone in the chapel to hear.

"My eyesight has been dimming slowly over the last several seasons. I wish to be able to see again as I once did," Cecile said.

Jehan saw the abbot smile. "Wonderful, wonderful," Ignace said. "And let me remind everyone here that the blessings only work on the faithful. I fear that one day someone will try to trick us into believing that the blessings didn't work. Those who would try such a thing are agents of the devil. They are those that would tear down this mighty work."

Then changing his voice to a softer, almost fatherly tone, Ignace asked Cecile, "Are you one of the faithful?"

"Oh, yes Abbot, yes!" she cried.

Ignace placed one hand on her head. He then looked up to the ceiling. After pausing for just a moment, he then proceeded with the blessing. Once it was completed, Jehan watched Cecile very carefully. She had closed her eyes during the ceremony, and now slowly opened them.

The look on her face was hard to read. Was it confusion? Perhaps she could see now better than before and the details were startling to her.

"My dear, you may return to your husband."

With what appeared to be a forced smile, Cecile nodded. She walked to where her husband stood with open arms. On the way to him, she bumped into the alter low—not hard, but enough that it caused her to stumble a little.

"Are you all right, sweetheart?" Luc asked.

"I'm fine," she said. "The power of the blessing left me a little overwhelmed is all."

Luc stepped toward her. "And can you see better?"

"Yes," she said, though without the conviction Jehan would have expected. "I am one of the Lord's faithful, so the blessing worked perfectly."

ଓଃ

Ignace found himself uncomfortable in his own Abbé, and he didn't care for it. He couldn't let Renaud be taken away and hung; that would send the wrong message to the people. They needed to feel safe within the walls of the Monastery, just as Renaud did. Yet, since he had granted sanctuary to the man, Renaud had been an annoyance and was bound to discover sooner or later how the diamond was made to shine.

These thoughts had troubled Ignace for quite some time now; it had been several weeks and the warmest part of the summer was behind them.

Soon it would turn cold and during the long winter, he would have Renaud inside for months. The very notion made him feel ill.

A light knock on the door interrupted his thoughts. "Yes?" Ignace asked, trying not at all to hide the irritation in his voice.

Brother Florent entered, head bowed to show proper respect. "Abbot, you asked me to stop by after my gate assignment."

Ignace remembered now he had done so. "Yes, come in and sit down."

Florent did as he was instructed.

"Do you know what we are doing here, what our calling is?" Ignace asked.

The monk frowned in thought for a moment. "We are here to do the Lord's work."

"And what work is that?"

Again the monk looked to be thinking deeply. "With the diamond divine, we are making the people better."

"That's right," Ignace said, trying to put into words what he was feeling. "With the use of the diamond divine, we are making the perfect man—one who will stand at St. Peter's Gate and be welcomed with open arms."

"It is a noble work," Florent said.

Ignace sat up, or at least he did the best he could in his deeply cushioned chair. "The devil is trying to stop us. We must send him to the fire. He is a crafty one—the master of half-truths and misguided notions. I fear we may have been led into temptation."

Florent looked surprised. "But, how?"

"Renaud," Ignace said darkly. "I believe he may be the devil's agent, here to disrupt this holy work. I have found myself uncomfortable in his presence."

Florent nodded. "I have sensed that as well. In fact…" He looked as if he was going to say more, but then decided against it.

"What? What is it you were going to tell me?" Ignace demanded.

While Florent's face was serene, there was something about the look in his eye that gave Ignace a reason to pause. It was almost mischievous.

"I think Renaud planned the murder, confession and request for sanctuary with the intention of stealing the diamond," Florent said.

Ignace shook his head. "No, the fear of ending up headless in the river would prevent that."

"For a rational person, perhaps," Florent said. "But does a rational man kill his wife and then hang her on the wall for display? I think not."

Brother Florent had a point. A *very* good point, in fact.

"And there's more," Florent added. "I've seen Renaud walking around the chapel after dark. It seems highly suspicious to me."

And then it happened again. A thought popped into Ignace's mind. It was like his other visions. He had contemplated a problem, and then miraculously an answer came to him. For a moment he was lost in his own thoughts, oblivious to everything around him. After a moment, the vision was completed and he became aware of Florent staring at him.

"Brother Florent," Ignace said. "I've had another vision. You are once again called upon to do the Lord's work.

"Go find Brother Jehan and tell him to go to the river. Then find Renaud and escort him down to the river as well. From there, let the Lord guide your actions."

Chapter 10

The sun had yet to rise, yet Christophe was already at work. It was a shipment day—one of three during the week which meant he had to be to work early. The shipments used to come during the day, but Didier feared that would cut into Christophe's sales time. His boss had carts full of items brought in from all around the region and was reaching out ever further into France. Today's shipment was one of the few that Didier actually supervised himself. It was odd that his employer would entrust him with the wares and money in the store each day, but certain shipments were too important, as Didier would say.

"Put it in the back room," Didier told the two burly men carrying the large crate. Christophe noticed the crate was made of finer wood and contained no markings on the exterior aside from a diamond-shaped symbol. He'd seen several of these crates over the last few months, but had never been allowed to open or unpack one.

One of the men tripped on the step into the shop and lost his balance. His companion was unable to compensate and the crate crashed to the ground. While it didn't burst open, it did crack enough that Christophe was able to catch a glimpse of a velvety purple shoe, like one worn by the women who were part of the abbot's new religion.

He quickly turned away, hoping that Didier hadn't noticed what he had seen.

"Idiots!" Didier screamed hysterically. "I'll make sure you lose your jobs over this if anything was damaged!"

Christophe heard the man who had fallen mumble, "I'm fine. Thanks for asking."

"What? What did you say?" Didier demanded.

"Nothing, sir," the other man said. He helped his coworker up. "We'll be more careful. We're truly sorry."

They picked up the box and headed toward the back. Christophe turned back around to see Didier standing at the door, his fists clenched. Then behind his employer, coming down the street, was another figure. Christophe instinctively stepped toward the door, trying to see who it was. Normally, no one was around this early, aside from those who were up to no good.

"Didier, behind you," Christophe whispered.

His boss glanced over his shoulder and then turned back to face Christophe. He didn't appear to be worried.

"Ah, that's just Odilon, my newest employee," Didier said.

Christophe wasn't sure what this meant. Was he being let go? He hit his quota almost every day, and on the days he didn't, he always made up for it the following day, as Didier demanded. His boss appeared to notice Christophe's reaction. "He's not here to replace you; he's here to help."

"Help? Help how?" Christophe asked, feeling relieved and anxious at the same moment. It was an odd sensation.

"I'll explain once he gets here," Didier said. He then waved Odilon to hurry up.

Odilon was not a large man; in fact, he stood a good head shorter than Christophe, which was saying something since Christophe was of average height at best. The other man had spiky yellow hair that was somehow neat and yet a bit unkempt at the same time. He approached with a big grin—so big that it seemed insincere.

"Hello, Didier," Odilon said when he arrived. He offered a hand to his new boss, who returned the shake. "And you must be Christophe," he said. He folded his arms and looked at Christophe from head to toe.

So, the new man was sizing him up, just as Christophe had done to him earlier.

The two men bringing in the supplies returned from the back room. They walked by Didier without saying a word and went to grab the next crate.

"Well met, Odilon." Christophe offered his hand in greeting. The shorter man took it, though it was akin to shaking hands with a dead fish.

"I've been hearing from certain customers that they've had to wait to be helped, and when they do get helped, they feel rushed because someone is waiting in line behind them," Didier said.

Christophe nodded. "Yes, ever since we began displaying the banner with the diamond, we've had many more customers, including several who are new to the area. I've been very busy, which, of course, is a good thing. It means we are selling more items and making you more money."

"But what good is that if the customers are complaining to others about how poorly they're being treated?" Didier asked. "Word spreads, you know. And if I am hearing people complain, then it means these same customers are complaining to other people in the town."

It seemed unfair for Didier to make this statement. Christophe was only one man, and yes, there were times when people would have to wait because he was helping someone else—but the person he was helping needed to feel like they were the most important person in the world. It seemed very much a contradiction. Perhaps Didier had finally seen this for what it was and that was the reason he decided to bring on more help. Christophe wondered how this would impact his daily quotas.

"I've been doing my best, and I'm glad you've hired extra help," Christophe said, trying to stay positive. "Between the two of us, I'm sure we'll be able to give more attention to each customer, and there will be shorter wait times."

Didier and Odilon looked at each other and then burst into laughter. Christophe wasn't sure what was so funny. The two men unloading the crates didn't laugh either as they walked by with another load.

His boss stopped laughing when the men started ascending the staircase to the loft. "Hey, where are you taking that crate?"

One of the men, the one who hadn't fallen before, responded, "We're taking it to the top. The back storage room is full."

Didier stomped his foot. "Then you must find a way to make it fit in the back. Crates like those need to be in the back room."

They were holding the same type of crate that had been dropped earlier—crates that Christophe wasn't allowed to open. The two men looked at each other, one of them rolled his eyes, and then they backed down the stairs.

Christophe watched them go and then asked, "What was so funny earlier?"

"Odilon isn't here to be another salesman," Didier said. He then poked a finger into Christophe's chest. "I have one of those already."

"Then why—"

The short man interrupted him. "I'm here to make sure the customers are treated properly. I'll be at the door the whole time."

"So, you'll be greeting them and entertaining them while they wait?" Christophe asked. This didn't make sense.

Odilon faced Didier. "He's not very bright, is he?"

Didier shook his head, then poked Christophe in the chest again. "I'll explain, and I'll use small words." This brought a chuckle from Odilon.

"Odilon is my cousin, and he just moved to the area to be close to the diamond divine," Didier explained. "He sold all his possessions to become a true follower of the Lord. As a member of His congregation, I graciously offered him a job. He is going to ensure the customers are happy."

"Forgive me," Christophe said, "but I'm still unclear on what he'll be doing."

Didier sighed. "He'll stand outside the store and as people leave, he'll ask them questions about the service they received."

"What kind of questions?" Christophe did not

like the direction this was headed.

"There will be four primary questions I'll ask them," the spiky-haired man said. "They are: 'Were you able to find exactly what you were looking for? Was Christophe knowledgeable enough to help you? Did Christophe exceed and surpass your expectations to treat you right? Is Christophe someone you can rely on all of the time?' From there, I'll ask them to grade the service they received on a scale of excellent, good, fair and poor."

"Isn't it a brilliant idea?" Didier again poked Christophe in the chest.

"I understand that we want our customers to be happy," Christophe said carefully. "I'll continue to do my best. But what happens if customers aren't happy? It's impossible to please everyone all the time."

"With an attitude like that, you can't," Odilon said. "Good thing you brought me aboard, cousin."

"The Lord says we must show mercy," Didier said. "Christophe, I understand you aren't perfect; if you were, you'd be with the Lord's chosen. Therefore, to show mercy, I'll allow one customer a day to rate you less than excellent in any one of the categories."

For the first time in Christophe's memory, he was at a loss for words.

Poking him in the chest a fourth time, Didier said, "But I expect everyone else to rate you as excellent in all of the questions.

"If they don't, the first thing that will happen is that you won't be paid any bonus coins you earn. If you haven't earned any bonus coins, you will be docked a coin for each person who says they didn't have an excellent experience in all four areas. Am I clear?"

Didier poked him in the chest one last time for emphasis. Christophe's reaction was to nod his head and bite his tongue. Only a few more weeks of this, and then I can get Rosette her blessing. I can do this. I can endure for her.

ᴕᴕ

Jehan walked into the chapel and was startled by what he saw. Standing on the top of the stairs next to the altar high was Abbot Ignace. Beside him, where people stood to be blessed, was Brother Florent. Ignace had one hand on the diamond divine and the other on Florent's head.

"Lucifer ex inferno clamat. Ne nos inducat in tentationem!" the abbot chanted. It was the same ceremony done to give blessings to members of the church, although it had been raining all day so no services had been held. When the abbot touched the stone, no light shone, even when giving the blessing.

After the blessing was completed, Brother Florent noticed Jehan standing just inside the chapel. "Ah, come to receive a blessing as well, Jehan?"

It hadn't occurred to Jehan to ask for a blessing, maybe because he was a monk and wasn't making donations. *Or perhaps I still don't have enough faith in the diamond divine.*

"I must say I'm surprised to see you here, Brother Jehan," Ignace said, "but also delighted you finally decided to ask for a blessing. You're the last monk to approach me."

The other monks had already done this and not said anything? Jehan wondered if this wasn't one of the abbot's tests, to see if the monks had enough faith to ask for a blessing.

He hadn't come to the chapel to be blessed; he had come to pray over how troubled he felt about Renaud being beheaded and thrown in the river. However, it seemed that both Florent and Ignace assumed he was here for other reasons. And why shouldn't he be blessed? *How will I know for sure if I don't try?*

"Yes, Abbot, I would," Jehan said.

"Then approach, Brother," Ignace intoned.

Jehan walked to the place where blessings were received. Before Ignace placed a hand on his head, the abbot said, "Just because you are a monk doesn't mean you are immune to the evil one's persuasion. The devil is calling us from hell. We need the Lord's help to not be led into temptation. Come. Come receive the blessing for pre-forgiveness for the upcoming week."

So that was why Florent was willing to visit the seedy taverns on the edge of town. He'd been pre-forgiven. What had Maximilien done with his blessing? Nothing out of the ordinary, aside from eating more and doing little else. He had been quite fat before, but was even more so now. Perhaps gluttony and sloth were his sins.

And Brother Bastien? Jehan hadn't seen him much, as the other monk's only job now aside from cooking was to position the reflective surfaces and open the hole in the ceiling when blessings were given. Bastien had always been a proud man and didn't like it when others received praise. It seemed envy and pride were his sins. As for Jehan himself, he'd always been tempted by the fairer sex, but felt bad about when he thought such things. Like Florent, it seemed lust was his sin, but so was despair.

But unlike Florent, Jehan wasn't quick to anger, so it seemed Florent also had the sin of wrath. And for the abbot? That was simple. It was greed and pride. Conceivably, the abbot was correct. Each man had his own sins with which he struggled.

Any further thoughts on the subject were interrupted when the abbot put one hand firmly on Jehan's head and started the chant.

The following day, the sun once again appeared in the sky. Though it was toward the end of the season, it would be a long, hot summer day. With the blessings done, Jehan was free to spend the afternoon as he wished.

He had lain awake most of the previous night. He had felt nothing out of the ordinary when he received his blessing yesterday. However, the abbot and Florent were both so passionate in their beliefs—or was it hopes? Was it a lack of faith on Jehan's part which caused his doubts? And what if it were true? He had been pre-forgiven of any sins he would commit this week, which inevitably led to thoughts of Ambre.

She had been at the Abbé today and had received a blessing of pre-forgiveness. When she left, she had caught Jehan's eye and winked at him. With all this in mind, he went down to the garden where she was working. He hid in the shadows, watching her. With her long black hair, eyes of fire, and her shapely body, he couldn't stop staring.

It was as if she sensed she was being watched, because she stopped her activities and turned to face where he was standing. He saw her smile, then she started to saunter toward him. His pulse started racing as she approached.

Part of his mind was telling him to run away before it was too late. Another part suggested that this was the test of faith he needed to prove to himself the divine nature of the diamond.

"Why hello, Brother Jehan," Ambre said smoothly. "What are you doing in the shadows?"

She walked up beside him and took him by the hand. "I saw you at the Abbé today, and I know you saw me. Once again, I've been pre-forgiven of my sins for the week."

"I received the same blessing recently," Jehan said, though his voice cracked when admitting it.

Her dark eyebrows shot up at the statement. "Brother Jehan, it's so hard to be holy. Would you like to be a man? I'll meet you tonight at the monastery wall, if you're there, we'll find out together. Since we are pre-forgiven, we will be blameless in the eyes of the Lord."

Temptation was here. Again, one part of his mind told him not to give in. He imagined the devil saying, "There's a place in Hell for the soul of Brother Jehan."

Another part of his mind nudged him, saying, "This is the test of your faith you needed. You need not fear. You are pre-forgiven."

He licked his lips and tried to speak, but no words came out. Ambre smiled again. She squeezed his hand tightly and said, "I've been waiting…" Saying no more, she returned to the garden.

Chapter 11

Lucien wiped the sweat off his brow. It was his third day as Fabrice's apprentice and so far, he had been enjoying it … aside from the heat.

"This is the worst part of the year," Fabrice said, after seeing that Lucien was dripping with sweat. "But I promise you, in the winter, you'll appreciate how the work keeps you warm. In the meantime, make sure you have plenty of water. Actually, go get us both a drink."

"Thank you, sir," Lucien said. "That would be nice."

Lucien removed his apron and gloves, then grabbed two bladders hung by the door. He had filled them first thing in the morning, but over the course of the day, he and Fabrice had emptied them.

"I'll need to go fill these." Lucien held them up for Fabrice to see. His mentor nodded and returned to his work.

Lucien stepped out into the heat of the mid-afternoon sun. He shifted the bladders to one hand so he could use the other to shade his eyes. There was a well not far from the woodworker's shop, so after getting his bearings, he headed in that direction.

"Hey! Lucien!" a familiar voice called out. It was Henri.

His older friend walked quickly to catch up to him. "So, you've gone and done it, eh? Become an official apprentice and all."

Lucien doubted Henri would take up a craft. Instead, he would continue to live off the profits made by his family's land and farms.

"It's really interesting work." Lucien realized he sounded defensive. "It's amazing to see how common wood is turned into something unique and beautiful."

Henri dismissed the comment with a wave of his hand. "Oh, I'm sure it is. But I've missed running around with you."

At that moment, Lucien realized that their other friend wasn't with Henri. "Where's Guy? He rarely leaves your side."

"Well, there was that nasty business of his father being accused of murder, and the death of Jocelyne. I heard that she was going to leave Renaud for Guy's father, and with her death, Guy's been staying by his father's side to comfort him. So, you see, I've had to be on my own."

He made it sound like it was some sort of burden he had to bear. Lucien wondered for a moment what it would be like not to have to worry about money. His own father seemed to be working himself to death to earn money for something, but neither his father nor mother would say what.

"Alas, I don't have time right now," Lucien said, motioning to the bladders he was holding.

"Perhaps tonight then," Henri countered. "I've been noticing some strange comings and goings around the Abbé, and I'm investigating them after the sun sets."

"What do you mean?"

Henri looked around and then whispered to Lucien, "I think there is a secret way in and out of the Abbé. There is the main gate, and the rear gate by the river, but I almost stumbled upon a monk coming out of a side entrance. Fortunately, he didn't see me."

"Which monk was it?" Lucien whispered back.

"I believe it was Brother Florent. I've seen him around the taverns on the edge of town and have often wondered how he got out of the Abbé so late at night."

Lucien frowned. "Answer me this, so what if you find another way into the Abbé? Certainly you've heard of the headless bodies found in the river. I hear they found another one just recently. It's best to stay away from that place, if you ask me."

His older friend looked offended. "I've been thinking about joining the congregation when I'm of age," Henri said stiffly. "But I'm curious about what goes on inside there and why monks are leaving late at night."

"You can go, my friend," Lucien said. "As for me, I want nothing to do with that place. Just be careful."

☙❧

Brother Jehan lay tossing and turning in his bed in the heat of the night. He had been struggling on what to do about Ambre. No matter how he tried, he couldn't stop thinking about her. He kept telling himself that it just felt wrong somehow, yet…

"Jehan," a soft voice called. He lay motionless to make sure what he heard wasn't his imagination.

For a moment, the only sounds that came from his window were the creatures that came out at night.

"Jehan," the voice called again. He went to his window and there she was in the clear moonlight. This was it. The test of his faith. He needed to choose: his inner feelings of uneasiness or to put faith in the diamond divine.

"I'll be right there," he heard his voice call back.

He had made his choice.

ଔ

Jehan went down the stairs from his upper room in the Abbé. His heart was pounding so loudly in his chest, he was sure it would wake up the abbot and the other monks. But he didn't see anyone as he crept to the secret passage in the side wall of the monastery. He understood that it had been added there when the Abbé was first built as a way for the monks to escape in case the town was overrun during one of the many wars that plagued the area.

With aid of the moonlight to guide him, he walked between the shrubberies that hid the small passageway through the wall. He ducked and walked through, meeting Ambre where they had agreed previously that day.

Ambre wore a tight-fitting dress with a low-cut neckline. She smiled when she saw him. She came toward him and pressed her body next to his.

He heard her whisper, "The sins of the flesh are too much to deny. Come, let's go to the shadows of the garden."

He had no words and simply let Ambre take him by the hand and lead him away from the Abbé. He was so enthralled by her that he didn't notice the figure of a young man watching them leave.

☙❧

Jehan woke with the dawn, for a moment unsure where he lay. He was outside; of that he was certain. Curled up next to him was Ambre. Memories of the previous night flooded over him. The experience had been as physically pleasant as anything he had ever felt, yet something was wrong.

He felt guilty.

He didn't know why. He searched out his mind to understand these feelings. He had put his faith in the diamond divine and the pre-forgiven blessing; then why did he feel the way he did?

For a moment, an image came to his mind. It was that of the devil laughing and angels crying over his soul.

☙❧

"Brothers," Ignace said to his four monks, "I've had another vision."

Three of them looked at him expectantly, while Brother Jehan seemed lost in his own thoughts. "Is something troubling you, Brother Jehan?"

The large monk's eyes appeared to refocus. "It is nothing, Abbot. Please, tell us about this vision."

"As you know, we've been extremely blessed since the diamond divine came to us," Ignace said. "Not only have we prospered, but the true followers have been blessed as well. Because the good word has spread, our town continues to grow, and we simply do not have space for all those who are petitioning for membership."

He motioned to the chapel around him. "This holy place isn't big enough for all the followers. In my vision, I stood in a chapel, more of a temple really, at least three times as large, with an upper balcony for all those who desired to follow the Lord's new religion. We have much gold in the treasury—enough to begin the process of building such a place."

He noticed Bastien frown a bit at the announcement. "And what of this wondrous vision causes you concern, Brother Bastien?"

"Not concern, Abbot," Bastien said, with his eyebrows lowered. "I was just planning on how best to proceed. I'm the obvious choice to be in charge of building this temple. While we have quite the supply of gold, we would still need more, in addition to the labor and supplies needed to build it."

"And you think the Lord has not revealed this to me as well?" Ignace's voice dripped with disdain. "The vision I had showed me people donating materials and their time in exchange for blessings from the diamond divine."

Bastien nodded. "Of course, Abbot. I beg your forgiveness."

"Granted."

"May I ask one other question?" Bastien asked carefully.

Ignace didn't respond verbally; he simply motioned for Bastien to ask.

"Did your vision show you when we are to start? With it getting late in the summer, and taking into account the additional time I'll need to prepare my plans, I think we would be ready by spring to begin construction."

That hadn't been part of the vision, but Bastien made a good point. He was the most adept at building, so Ignace would give him leave to proceed as he thought best. "It is as you say, Brother."

"And then there is the other matter we must deal with," Brother Florent said.

Ignace lifted his head a bit and looked down his nose at Florent. "I was about to discuss that. You need to practice patience, Brother Florent."

The monk looked angry for a moment, but then composed himself. "Yes, Abbot."

"Until we get this larger chapel—nay, temple—built, we need to address how we will serve all those who seek guidance and blessings from the Lord. We have many new people petitioning to become members and we simply don't have the room for them. In addition, we have those who would pay just to witness the blessings, even if they aren't members themselves."

Ignace sighed dramatically. "I know there are those members that will frown upon having the common person on the street allowed in, but it will increase the gold needed for the temple, and in return, they will be given a sense of hope that one day they can receive the blessings. Of course, they will have to pay at the gate for admittance into the chapel."

He pointed to Bastien. "Before working on the temple plans, I need you to have a row of stone benches placed against the back wall of the chapel. This is where those who just want to watch will sit—separate from the members, but still in the chapel."

Brother Bastien nodded. "It will be done."

ଓଃ୭୦

Odilon shook his head while examining his notes. "Oh, Christophe, this has not been a good day for you. Oh no, not at all."

It seemed to Christophe that Odilon actually enjoyed reporting bad news.

"You only helped seven customers all day," his co-worker said. "And none of them were very happy."

Christophe pointed to the heavy rain outside. "It's been like this for two days straight. People don't want to leave their homes, let alone go to shops, in weather like this. I'd be grumpy as well if I had to go out in this storm."

Odilon glanced up from his notes. "But you *did* have to go through this storm to come to work. No wonder the people weren't happy—you just admitted that you are grumpy."

"I—" Christophe started to say, but then held himself back. He was just days away from having enough coin to join the membership of the new religion and pay for Rosette's blessing. *I can make it.*

"You what?" Odilon asked.

Christophe lowered his eyes. "I will do better."

"You need to. This is the second day in a row

you've not hit your quota and have gotten less than perfect responses from people who have shopped. I'm sure Didier has people lined up to take your job when you fail."

So, it was a matter of when *and not* if *now?* "We'll have a better day tomorrow," Christophe said, trying to convince himself as much as the other man.

The rain was so thick and heavy, Christophe could hardly see the road ahead of him as he made his way home. It was unusually cool for this time of year. Autumn had begun, with the leaves just now starting to change colors, but it felt more like late autumn heading into winter.

Winter.

A sudden thought came to his mind. Had Rosette gone out in this weather? She must have known better than to go out into the cold. But today was the day she went shopping for food. Surely she would put it off a day so as not to risk. . .

With no regard that he couldn't see far ahead of him, Christophe started running as fast as he could toward his home.

He found Rosette bundled up in every blanket they owned. Still, she was shivering. Christophe didn't even need to ask if she had gone out into the raging storm. It wasn't the stocked pantry that gave it away; rather, it was how her body reacted to getting so cold and wet.

"I honestly thought I would be fine. It's only autumn," she said through chattering teeth.

Lucien was by her side. He appeared to be on the edge of tears.

"I've got some water warming for broth,"

Lucien said. "That's always helped, right?"

Christophe smiled at his son and wife. "That's right."

He then used his bravest voice. "Let me change out of these wet clothes and then we'll get your mother all warmed up, inside and out. She'll be fine."

His son nodded then stood. "I'll check on the water."

Quickly, Christophe stripped off the soaked clothes and changed into something warm and dry. By the time he was done, Lucien was back at his mother's side, saying, "It won't be much longer now."

Christophe finished making the broth and brought it over to Rosette in a bowl, along with some bread. Carefully, he and Lucien helped her finish the food. The broth seemed to help, as she was shivering less, but she still was cold to the touch. Both Rosette and Christophe convinced Lucien to go to bed, that she would be fine now.

After making sure their son was asleep, Christophe curled up next to his wife. "Rosette, my sweet Rosette," he said, stroking her cheek. He tried not to flinch when he felt how cold she was.

"My dear husband," she said, her voice soft and raspy. "I'm sorry. I shouldn't have—"

He put a finger to her lips to quiet her. "No need to apologize. You'll be fine."

She looked at him, her eyes conveying sadness. "I'm not so sure, Christophe. It's never been this bad before."

"I'll have Lucien buy some of those special herbs first thing in the morning," he said. "I'll have him make some herbal tea for you. That's always helped. I'll make sure he's here with you tomorrow. I'll send word to Fabrice that Lucien won't be in."

"Christophe, why don't you stay with me instead?" she asked.

"Rosette," he said gently, "I'm so close to earning enough money to get you a blessing of health. Just a few more days and I'll be able to afford it."

For a moment, she didn't speak. She simply looked at him. Then finally she said, "You honestly believe in the diamond divine, don't you?"

"I do. I have to believe that the diamond will work. I don't know what else to do to prevent you from getting ill each winter. You mean everything to me, Rosette. In fact, I've been working on a song for you."

At this, her eyes sparkled. "You've been writing songs again?" Was that hope that shone in her eyes?

"Not songs as much as a song—this song for you."

"Will you sing it for me?" she asked, her eyelids now starting to droop.

"It's not quite done yet."

Her eyelids were closed now. "Will you at least tell me what it's about?"

"Yes, my love. It's about the first time we met. You remember, don't you?"

The corners of her mouth curled up. "Yes… it was a magical night. Please, sing me just a little part of it."

Christophe gazed on the love of his life. Even with all the struggles at work, she was the reason he stayed in the fight. It was all for her.

"All right, I will," he said.

He cleared his throat, and then as tenderly as he could, he sang the opening lines to the song.

"I've never seen you looking so lovely as you did tonight, I've never seen you shine so bright…"

Chapter 12

Constable Gaubert had his arms folded and was scowling at Abbot Ignace and Brother Florent. He stood just inside the gates of the Abbé, and had once again used threats to get an audience. This is something Ignace couldn't let continue.

"You're honestly telling me that you know nothing about how Renaud ended up headless in the river?" Gaubert asked.

"I didn't say that." Ignace scowled right back at the constable. "What I said was that we know those who try to steal the diamond divine end up with the same fate."

The thickly built man in front of Ignace sighed, obviously frustrated. "You gave Renaud sanctuary here in the Abbé St. Pierre, did you not?"

"You know full well that I did," Ignace retorted. "Or do you not remember that you were standing in almost the same exact spot when it was granted?"

"Do not twist my words against me," Gaubert said. "Yes, I remember the event. And the last time I saw him alive was when I left him here with you. So imagine my surprise when I get a report of his headless body found on one of the riverbanks close by. Since he was under your protection, it's only logical that you would know something about how he ended up there."

Ignace was already upset because the constable had once again made demands to see him, but now the man crossed the line and was making accusations. Gaubert seemed to forget who he was dealing with.

"You want to use *logic*?" Ignace asked. "Even though as men we cannot begin to understand all the ways of the Lord, we'll use logic for now. Renaud was in the Abbé. The diamond divine is protected by the Lord, and those who try to steal it end up dead in the river, headless. Renaud was found without his head in the river, so *logically*, he tried to steal the diamond and suffered the consequence of his poor choice."

Gaubert rubbed his eyes. "But how is the diamond protected? Do you hire an assassin? Does one of the members of your congregation do it for you? Does the Lord himself come down and chop off the person's head and then throw the body into the river?"

"Blasphemy!" Ignace roared. He sensed Florent tense up next to him, but the monk knew better than to act without orders. "Again, you dare to say such things in this holy place."

Gaubert folded his arms again and smirked. "And what will you do about it? Have the Lord come down and cut off my head as well?"

The constable had gone too far. Yet, he had been given his assignment by someone to keep the peace after the war. Certainly as abbot of this new and growing religion, Ignace could influence Gaubert's leaders to remove the man. But maybe not in time before Gaubert did something to jeopardize his position as the Lord's chosen leader.

And, if he were to have Florent take care of the constable, his replacement could be even more difficult to deal with.

Once again, a solution popped into Ignace's mind. It was just like his other visions. When he was faced with a problem, an answer came to him. He thought it out to its conclusion, staring into the sky.

"Ignace?" Gaubert asked. The fact that he didn't use his proper title wasn't lost on the abbot. "Is this your plan? To ignore me?"

"No," Ignace said, his voice calm. "Constable Gaubert, the Lord himself has given me a vision."

Gaubert looked skeptical.

"He is saddened that your eyes are closed to the wondrous events that are happening here at the Abbé St. Pierre. You could be one of His greatest followers, instead, you have let the devil into your heart—no doubt from all those years of fighting and killing in the war."

"Ignace—" Gaubert started to say.

He continued as if the constable hadn't said anything. "You have been assigned to this post not to tear down the Lord's work, but to build it up. If you continue down your current path, the Lord will replace you with one who will open their eyes."

"Is that a threat?" The constable glanced between him and Brother Florent. Gaubert put his hand on the hilt of his sword. Florent set his feet, as if he was ready to spring into action.

Ignace stayed calm as he spoke. "It's not a threat. It's a consequence from your actions. If you fight against me, your leaders will have you removed and sent somewhere where you will deal with much greater dangers than are found here."

For the first time since Gaubert demanded to see the abbot, the constable's resolve appeared to waiver.

"What do you know of my leaders?" he asked, his voice less confident than before.

"Certainly you have seen how the word of the Lord has spread and how His influence is growing. Powerful men are making pilgrimages to my Abbé for blessings. Men like these would certainly know your leaders and could tell them of the troubles you are bringing to the church," Ignace said. "So, Constable Gaubert, I invite you to open your eyes. Don't let the devil win. Let the Lord bless you."

Gaubert's face paled. Ignace wasn't sure where the constable could be sent that would cause such a reaction, but certainly the Lord did when he gave Ignace the vision.

"I'll take my leave now, Abbot," Gaubert said. He turned to exit the Abbé.

Ignace nodded. "A wise choice."

❧

Lucien's head jerked up. He had dozed off again, and he chided himself for doing so. He hadn't left his mother's side all night, and had been so worried about her that he had slept little. It was now catching up to him. His father had to go into work early, it was a shipment day, but as soon as he could, Lucien was going to buy the herbs for the tea.

She had been shivering off and on all night, but seemed to be resting better, with only a slight tremble now and then. He didn't want to wake her—she needed her rest.

Lucien stood and went to the window to gauge

how far the sun had gone up in the sky. It wouldn't be long now before he could go, though he didn't want to leave her side.

Ever since he was young, he remembered his mother getting sick during the first cold spell of the season. But it had never come so early, nor had it affected her this badly. He returned to her side and listened to her breathe. It was slow, but it was there.

He sat there for a moment longer, until he couldn't wait anymore to buy the herbs. His father had left him three coins, the amount to get what he needed. He clutched them in his hand and set off toward the market district.

The woman that sold the herbs was on the outskirts. Whereas La boutique de désirs—where his father worked—was in the center of town, the merchants who sold produce and the like stayed closer to the fields. Unfortunately, this meant that Lucien had to walk clear across town to make the purchase. He felt like running, but that might get the attention of some of the ruffians that still walked the streets now and again. No, it was better to keep walking and blending in with the crowd.

There was still a chill in the air, even though the sun was out. He finally spotted his destination, and quickened his pace a little. The woman who sold the herbs was not pleasant to look at. Her teeth were yellow and rotting in her mouth, and she had dark splotches covering her leather-like skin.

"Eh, whatcha be wanting then?" She looked at Lucien as if he was a nuisance.

Lucien pointed to the herb. "I need some of those to make a tea for my sick mother."

"Those, eh? That'll be five coins, then." She

held her gnarled hand.

"Five? These have always cost only three," Lucien said, startled.

The woman shrugged. "Prices have gone up. I'm saving to get a blessing from the diamond divine, as are the rest of the merchants. Blessings aren't cheap, so we need to make more money."

"Please," Lucien said. He began to cry. "My mother is very sick and I need these herbs. All I have is three coins."

"Well, if you truly love your mother, you better bring me two more coins so you can get what you want. As of right now, you are just another poor boy telling me some sad story to get me to lower my prices. Be off with you."

☙❧

Didier greeted Odilon at the door and spoke to him in a hushed voice. Christophe watched as the two men glanced inside at him. Odilon was motioning furiously with his hands, and whatever was being said, it caused Didier to scowl.

It had been a fairly decent morning, sales wise, and if it kept steady in the afternoon, he had a good chance of not only meeting his quota for the day, but would make up for the last two days where he'd been short.

His boss entered the shop and said, "Word has it people are still finding that your treatment of them could be better."

This honestly surprised Christophe. The people he had helped this morning had all left happy, from what he could tell. "What have you heard?"

"Odilon said one of the customers reported

you didn't exceed and surpass what they expected."

Christophe felt a headache coming on. "And what was their definition of 'exceed and surpass', eh? It seems to be something different for each person."

Didier threw his hands up in the air. "How do *I* know what they expected? I just know that you didn't do it!"

Out of the corner of his eye, he saw his son, Lucien, at the shop's entrance. Odilon had a hand on the boy's chest, trying to keep him from coming in. Christophe looked over at his son and asked, "Lucien, what are you doing here? You should be home with your mother. Is she still resting?"

"Yes, but—" Lucien began.

Christophe couldn't think straight. His son knew better than to come here when he was supposed to be home. He shook a finger at him. "Not now, son. Do as you are told and get home to your mother. She needs you by her side. Am I clear?"

Lucien looked like he wanted to say something else, but Didier stopped him. "You heard him, now go!"

Lucien bowed his head and left. The unpleasant shop owner turned his attention back to Christophe. "How are you supposed to run my shop if you can't even run your own household?" Didier taunted.

Christophe balled his hands into fists. He'd not been this angry in a long time, yet he almost had the coin he needed for Rosette. He couldn't throw that away now. He took in a deep breath and said, "I will do better to 'exceed and surpass' with the customers."

Didier looked as if he was going to rebuke him some more, but then turned instead to talk to Odilon.

While Christophe straightened some items on a shelf, he listened to Didier brag about his latest kill—a white bird. Though when he went to retrieve it, all he could find was blood on the ground. His boss surmised that some wild beast must have gotten to it first, such was his bad fortune.

Despite all that was happening in Christophe's life at the moment, Didier's tale inspired a few lines to a poem, or perhaps a song, to come to Christophe's mind.

ଔ଼

Lucien hurried home, this time running as fast as he could, regardless of what attention this might bring upon him. He couldn't believe his father had dismissed him without hearing what he had to say. It wasn't like his father to do such things. He wondered what Didier had done to cause him to act in such a manner. Perhaps his mother had a few more coins stashed somewhere so he could get the five he needed.

He entered the house and went to his parents' room where his mother appeared to be resting peacefully. At least she no longer had the shakes. It hurt him to see her suffer like that.

"Mother," he said softly as he approached.

She didn't respond. He moved closer, and placed one hand on her shoulder. "Mother," he said again. He went to gently wake her when he realized something.

She wasn't moving at all.

Lucien raced around to the other side of the bed. Her skin was pale and her eyes were closed.

"Mother!" He shook her by the shoulder forcefully. Despite all he tried, she wouldn't wake. He leaned in closer and noticed she wasn't breathing. If she wasn't breathing that meant...no! It couldn't be!

But no matter how hard he tried to deny it, he knew deep inside that his mother was gone.

☙❧

An eastern wind blew harshly, yet Christophe barely noticed. Not only was it blowing fiercely, but it was bitterly cold. He should be freezing, but he actually felt nothing at all. He had been numb ever since he had come home to find that his wife had died. His son hadn't left her side once he had found her—and they both stayed with her through the night. While Lucien cried openly for the first time in many seasons, Christophe sat motionless.

He had spent so much time and put up with so much unfairness to earn a blessing of health for Rosette, but it was all for naught. When she needed him, really needed him, he wasn't there. Lucien told him about not having enough for the herbs, and that is why he came to see him at the shop. Would they have helped? They always had in the past—but would it have been enough to preserve her life? He didn't know.

There were many things he wasn't sure about now. How would he live without her? Would Lucien blame him for her death? Would he ever be able to forgive himself? So many unknowns.

However, there was something that he did know for sure. And with that singular thought in his mind, he continued through the eastern wind to La boutique de désirs. It was one of those mornings where Didier was personally supervising the incoming shipment.

Lately, Odilon had been coming in early as well, and Christophe noticed the his boss's cousin had on gloves worn by members of Ignace's congregation.

"About time you got here." Didier scowled. He hopped from one foot to another to stay warm.

"You aren't off to a good start today," Odilon said. He was bundled up in a thick cloak, and mist could be seen when he breathed out. "You better not let this impact how you treat customers."

Christophe stood in front of the two men who treated him so poorly. Instead of feeling angry, he felt something else: pity.

These men were reaching for something that wasn't there. Yet, they couldn't see that and he doubted anything he said would change their minds.

"I promise you that no one will complain about my service today," Christophe said, his voice showing no emotion.

Odilon laughed out loud and slapped Didier on the shoulder. "Did you just hear the same thing I did? That's quite the commitment to keep. How can you even think to make such a statement?"

He looked Odilon in the eye, then deliberately turned and looked at Didier. Christophe's facial expression was blank. He then turned and started to walk back toward his house.

"Where are you going?" Didier sounded angry.

Christophe stopped. He turned his head and

then looked back over his shoulder. "I'm saying good-bye to La boutique de désirs. I'm saying good-bye to you and Odilon. I'm saying good-bye to it all."

"You can't leave!" Didier screamed. "Who's going to sell all these items we just got in?"

Christophe continued walking back to his house, ignoring the threats, demeaning comments and then the eventual begging that came from his former boss.

Chapter 13

"Fix me a drink, make it a strong one," Gaubert said to the barkeep.

"As you say, Constable," came the reply from Jourdain, the establishment's owner.

The tavern was unusually full tonight, which made Gaubert suspicious. Then again, as constable, he was suspicious of just about everything. For whatever reason, people were nervous around him, and were almost always hedging the truth, as if by doing so, they would be in less trouble with the law. Therefore, he learned to doubt what most people told him. Except for the threat from Abbot Ignace. In that, he had no doubts. The man was powerful and dangerous. Gaubert wondered if the abbot knew how much power he wielded. From his time in the war, Gaubert had seen men of power get soldiers to do their bidding—and often it was out of fear for their lives. But the abbot was different—he honestly thought that he had been getting visions from the Lord. And people believed him.

Gaubert had little use for the abbot's religion. But he knew that Ignace had powerful men listening to him—men that could get him reassigned to one of the less prosperous areas where constables were treated poorly, and were often killed by the locals who were still fighting a war that had supposedly ended.

He saw little choice but to do as Abbot Ignace said, though it bothered him that he was forced into this position.

"Here you go, Constable," Jourdain said.

He took the mug from the barkeep. "Why are there so many people here tonight?"

Jourdain's bushy eyebrows rose. "You didn't hear? Christophe is performing."

"Christophe…" Gaubert said. "Didn't his wife die recently? Also, wasn't he fired by Didier?"

"That's him," Jourdain said. "However, to hear Christophe tell it, he quit—though Didier wants people to believe he was fired."

Gaubert took a sip of his drink. It was strong, just like he asked. He felt it burn as it went down his throat. "Why quit a good job like that? From what I've seen, Didier is very successful."

"Probably something to do with his wife dying. Events like that can change a man."

The tavern owner made a good point. Several of the men he served with during the war were completely different afterwards. "So, you're telling me he quit working for Didier and is now working for you?"

"Not really working *for* me." Jourdain frowned. "He had performed here in the past, and was a crowd favorite, but then stopped for quite a while. People would ask when he was coming back and I saw more and more of my customers leave to visit some of the more, let's say, less reputable taverns on the edge of town. When he came to me and said he would be willing to perform here again, I saw it as a way to bring in more business."

"But something's different this time, isn't it?"

Gaubert asked, hearing it in the other man's voice.

"Yes," Jourdain said. "Christophe drives a hard bargain. Whereas he performed before for next to nothing, he's now got me to agree to split any coin made while he is here—and he keeps all the tips."

Gaubert was startled. "And you agreed to this?"

This time, Jourdain smiled. "Well, wait until you hear him for yourself and then you tell me if I made a good deal or not.

Over the next little while, more people came into the tavern, filling every nook. People were standing and leaning on the railings of the second story that overlooked the common area. Next to the fireplace was a little stage of sorts, really not much more that an elevated platform about knee high. The only object on the stage was a small stool.

Gaubert kept nursing his drink while he waited for Christophe to arrive. The people around him seemed to grow more excited with each passing moment.

Finally, Christophe came from a room just off the side of the stage. He was a man of medium height and build, with dark hair that was just starting to thin. Christophe held a lute in one hand and waved to the crowd with the other. The people began cheering even before he said a word.

"I'd like to thank you all for coming," Christophe said after they had calmed down enough for him to be heard. He sat on the stool. "I've missed singing for you all." There were more cheers. "As you may have heard, my sweet Rosette died recently," Christophe said. "Her burial was very hard for me, and I thank all of you who attended and showed your support."

The tavern had gotten very quiet now. Gaubert was amazed how this man was able to get and keep their attention.

"I promise to play for you all your favorites, as well as a few less known, and at least two new songs," Christophe said. "I'd like to start with one I recently wrote. This is called *Songbird.*"

The song's lyrics were sweet and beautiful. He gathered it was about a songbird who sang so beautifully that it enchanted any who heard her. The most powerful line to Gaubert was, "And when she sings from the high walls of Heaven, will the angels cry like me?"

The crowd was completely mesmerized by the performance and applauded loudly when he finished the song. Gaubert noticed most of the women and many of the men were in tears because of the performance, and showed their appreciation by generously adding coins to the jar set aside for tips.

Christophe then allowed, and encouraged, people to visit the barkeep before he started his next song. Gaubert was all but shoved out of the way as the crowd did just that.

The constable considered Christophe for a moment. The song he performed was unlike any he had heard. There was an underlying message there—one that the common person probably didn't grasp.

Like the abbot, Christophe had the ability to play on people's emotions. But unlike the abbot, there was something sincere about the man. Gaubert was leery of any man that could have such an impact on the people. This Christophe was someone he would need to watch carefully.

ଔ

The night sky was clear and the air, crisp. Christophe and Lucien were sitting on a hill not far from their house, a place they would go often when Lucien was younger. From here, there was a nice view of the region as well as the sky. It was late, much later than Christophe usually let Lucien stay up. Ever since he had quit working for Didier, Christophe had been awake well past dark and arising after his son had already left to go work with Fabrice. At first, it was because he couldn't sleep from the grief of losing his wife. But over the last several weeks, it had been because he found the quiet moments in the evening the best time to write and practice his songs. Lucien didn't seem to mind—if anything, he loved hearing his father sing.

"I miss mother," Lucien hugged his knees.

Christophe put an arm around his son. "I miss her, too."

"Do you think she misses us?" Lucien asked.

Christophe felt the familiar feeling of grief starting to build inside him. "What do you think?"

Lucien pulled his knees in even closer to his chest. "I'm not sure. At the funeral, the abbot said that only those who donated enough to the church would be with their loved ones again. But the cost for that seems like an awfully large amount of money."

It had cost nearly a quarter of his savings to pay for a proper burial for Rosette, which included a mandatory donation to the church.

The abbot's words still echoed in Christophe's mind. "To Thee, O Lord, we give thanks for all. We thank Thee for the diamond divine and the power it gives me to bless the people. As we put this woman into the cold ground, we ask Thee to watch over her soul until which time she can be blessed with eternal life."

The message was clear. Rosette wouldn't be allowed into heaven until Christophe was able to get a blessing from the diamond divine. And even then, she wouldn't be allowed to be with her loved ones unless that blessing was granted as well.

"I have some good news about that, son," Christophe said. He squeezed his son tighter. "The money I made at the tavern tonight was equal to what I made in a week for Didier." Christophe wished he had known he could make this much while he was working for that awful man. "Jourdain did an excellent job promoting my return. In a matter of time, I can save up for blessings for our whole family."

"You really believe that the diamond divine has that kind of power, don't you?" Lucien asked.

"I do," Christophe replied. "I know your mother had doubts, but I, for one, am willing to show faith in it. If it can truly bring us together as a family beyond this world, I am willing to make the needed sacrifices."

Lucien didn't say anything for a moment. Instead, he tilted his head up and looked up at the night sky.

"Guy's father, Claude, doesn't believe in the diamond, nor the way the abbot describes the afterlife," his son said.

It wasn't the first time Lucien had shared some of the painter's odd beliefs. Instead of dismissing them out of hand, Christophe always listened to what his son said so they could talk about it.

"What does Claude say then?"

"He says that the stars in the sky are the souls of the people who die," Lucien said. "And that they are looking down upon us."

"And what do you think?" Christophe tried to hide the doubt in his voice.

Lucien took in a deep breath, and then exhaled. "I'm not sure. If it *is* true, I think there's a new star in heaven."

cs&o

"Timing is everything," Ignace said to Bastien. "Twice, recently, you've been late in letting the light shine on the diamond."

The monk bowed his head during the rebuke. *At least he still knows his place.* "This is the first time we've let commoners in to watch, so there can be no mistakes. Are you clear on this Brother Bastien?"

"Very clear, Abbot."

"Be off then, the crowd is ready."

With that, Bastien exited the abbot's chambers leaving Ignace alone. The abbot wondered if this was the same frustration the Lord felt when people didn't do as they were told. It's no wonder He brought the flood—there were times the abbot would do the same.

Ignace found comfort knowing he was doing the Lord's will. Yet, with all the donations of food and coin that let him live a comfortable life, he still had the burden of leading this new religion.

Surely he would be rewarded immensely in the

afterlife. Any bothers and frustrations he felt now would be worth it—at least they had better be.

He took in a deep breath, made sure his purple velvet robe was free of any crumbs from the bread he had just eaten, then exited his chambers into the chapel.

The usual members of the church sat in the front rows, dressed in proper attire—the correct gloves for the men, shoes for the women. In fact, all the pews were filled with members of the church, some frowning a little. Ignace knew that allowing non-members to observe from the back of the chapel wasn't going to be popular with some of the more devout people. But they didn't have to like it, they just needed to do what they were told.

The abbot walked up to the altar mid and nodded solemnly to the congregation. "I have an announcement to make before we begin today," Ignace said. "After winter ends, work will begin on a new building for us to worship in. It will be so magnificent that calling it a chapel would be inappropriate. It will be a temple, like one that hasn't been built in generations. It will be the center of the new holy land, and over time, will far exceed anything found in Paris or Rome. And you, my people, will be given the honor to help—giving you a prominent place in history."

Excited whispers and expressions came from the truly worthy in the crowd.

Even those that were not members, but had paid the tariff at the gate for entry, seemed to be caught up in the excitement of the proclamation. All except one man.

He was dressed in a dark robe, and sat up

straight, unlike the commoners who tended to slump. The man looked somewhat familiar to Ignace, though he couldn't say why. While those around him seemed to be energized by his vision, this man was frowning. Ignace couldn't dwell on the man now, he had duties to perform.

"And now, Brother Jehan will bring up the first member to be blessed," Ignace said.

The large monk escorted the beautiful Ambre to the altar low. She placed her offering. "I wish for a blessing of a week's pre-forgiveness," she stated.

Ignace nodded and motioned her forward. He saw her wink at Jehan and then noticed the monk was blushing.

There was enough sunlight to allow Ignace to complete the rest of the blessings for the day. Once the service had concluded, people exited the chapel, many whispering excitedly about the news Ignace had shared.

The man in the dark robe didn't move from his seat until everyone else had left the chapel. Ignace didn't like how the man continued to frown and stare at him. Perhaps he was a thief or assassin, here to take the diamond. If that was the case, he was in for an unpleasant surprise.

"Brothers Jehan and Florent," Ignace said. "It seems we have a visitor that is unaccustomed to our ways. Please help him to the door."

As the two monks moved toward the man, he stood. "There is no need for that, Ignace," the man said. The stranger's voice was familiar.

The abbot wondered, *Who is this man that would address me so casually?*

"Then, pray tell, why do you remain behind

when it is clearly time to leave?" Ignace asked.

The man grimaced. "You honestly don't remember me, do you Ignace?"

"Should I?"

Florent continued to move slowly toward the man, while Jehan stopped and watched.

"I would think so," the stranger said. "After all, we did attend seminary together."

And then Ignace placed the man. He was Charles—an ambitious man who had moved up the ranks of the church quickly.

"Of course, Charles," Ignace said, putting on his best smile. "It seems the years have changed you."

"Or perhaps it is your sight that has changed." There was no hint of humor in Charles's voice.

"Perhaps." Ignace stepped down from the alter high as he asked, "And what brings you here to the Abbé St. Pierre?"

Charles lifted his arms and motioned around the chapel. "Did you think word of your actions here wouldn't reach your superiors?"

Ah, so that was it. They'd heard of the diamond divine and wanted it for themselves. Ignace felt his pulse start to race and his face felt like it was burning. "My superiors? Why Charles, I only have one superior—the Lord himself. And of course He knows my actions. He is guiding me."

"What you are saying Ignace is blasphemy," Charles spat out. "Are you renouncing your position in the church?"

Ignace took a step forward and motioned for Florent to stop his continued movement toward Charles.

"Did Moses renounce the church when he was chosen by the Lord to lead his people? No. And yet, this is what you ask of me. It is *you* that speaks blasphemy. You heard my announcement during the service. I have been chosen of the Lord to lead people into the light. Until you recognize and acknowledge that, you have no business here."

Before Charles could respond, Ignace addressed his monks. "Brother Florent, Brother Jehan, see that this man leaves the Abbé and doesn't return until he is ready to become a true follower."

Ignace turned his back on the man and headed toward his room, ignoring Charles's disparaging comments as the monks forced him out of the chapel.

ଔ

A knocking on the door broke Christophe's concentration. He had been working on his next song, one he hoped to perform that night. He almost had it, but there was something missing—something in the feeling and message he was trying to convey.

He set his lute on the table and went to the door. After opening it, he was surprised to see who had paid him a visit. Didier stood there, looking uncomfortable in his own skin.

"Christophe," he said in greeting, though his tone and demeanor seemed to indicate he was not happy to see his former employee.

"Didier," Christophe responded, making no effort to let him in. The other man appeared to notice and glowered.

"I've come here to offer you your old job

back," Didier said, as if it was the hardest thing in the world to say.

Christophe was stunned by the statement. "I've no interest in returning, Didier." With that, Christophe went to close the door.

"Wait!" Didier said. He then looked around as if to see if anyone was watching. "Wait."

"What is it?"

The man before him, the self-proclaimed great hunter and prosperous merchant, bowed his head. "I'll give you a large bonus to return. Sales have been down significantly since Odilon took over your position. And there have been nothing but complaints from the customers since you left."

Christophe wondered if perhaps Didier would give him enough to pay for the blessings he needed for him and his family. "What are your terms?"

A glimmer of confidence appeared in Didier's eyes. "The bonus will be a week's worth of pay. You will, of course, be subject to the same expectations as before."

A week's worth of pay—the same amount he earned in one night at the tavern. Christophe considered the man before him. Here was this man of worldly wealth, yet with all his money, he couldn't buy what he wanted, and he couldn't understand why not.

It was at that moment Christophe realized the missing piece to his song.

"Didier," Christophe said, "do not come to my house again. Ever."

And with that, Christophe closed the door.

Once again, the tavern was filled to bursting. This was Christophe's third show this week, and each time, he had received a wonderful response. Jourdain had hired young men to go around town to spread the word of his performances—that, and word of mouth from those who had already seen him play—brought in large crowds. He had even heard that half again as many people had to be turned away for there was simply not enough room.

He opened with a couple of songs that were crowd favorites—the first of his own writing, the second, a traditional folk song from the area.

After the applause of appreciation from the second song, Christophe announced, "Thank you all for coming!" The crowd roared in approval. "I'd now like to perform a brand new song for you—one that I hope you enjoy. It's called *The Tower.*"

Again the people in the tavern applauded and then quieted down so they could hear him.

He strummed the first chord on his lute and then began to sing.

The song told the story of a great lord who enjoyed hunting. One day, he shot a white bird. However, when he went to find his kill, he instead found a beautiful woman. Her hand was hurt. The lord became instantly obsessed with her.

He offered her riches to come with him. Instead, she said she would go with him on the condition the lord would stop hunting—he had no need.

Instead, the lord bound her and took her to a tower. When he did, thunder and lightning filled the heavens, and the birds left the sky.

Each day, the lord would visit her. The only

thing she would say was, "Leave them in peace."

But the lord enjoyed hunting too much. He refused to give it up.

One day he went to visit her, but only found a single white feather on the floor. She was gone.

At that moment, the lord understood. He spent the rest of his life aching for the woman, begging her to come back. But all he had was her memory.

After completing the song, the crowd was silent. Christophe noticed many were wiping away tears—even Jourdain was using his apron to dry his eyes. The best day working for Didier paled in comparison to what he felt now.

Christophe had found his calling.

Chapter 14

"Brother Maximilien, wake up!" Jehan said to the fat monk. Maximilien had gotten so large that the seat at the Abbé's gate no longer supported him. A special bench, wide enough to sustain his girth, had replaced the chair.

Jehan grabbed Maximilien's shoulder and shook it, trying to get his fellow monk to stop snoring.

"Huh? What? Is it time to eat?" Maximilien asked upon waking.

"No," Jehan said through clenched teeth. "It's time to let the people in."

Brother Maximilien raised both his chubby arms above his head and let out a mighty yawn. "Already?" He then looked to the sky and said, "These shorter days are confusing me. It seems like we just get up when it's time to go to bed again."

"The abbot is ready! Do you want to keep him waiting?" Jehan asked. He looked over his shoulder and saw Brother Florent watching them from the chapel door.

Maximilien tried to get up, but didn't succeed. He tried again, this time rocking back and forth to get momentum. Jehan sighed and grabbed the man by an elbow and helped him get to his feet. Even though Jehan was big and strong, helping Maximilien up was difficult.

"Thank you, Brother," Maximilien said once he steadied himself by putting a hand on the gate.

Jehan motioned to lift the latch. "Remember, as long as they are wearing the proper gloves or shoes, they're let right in. Everyone else must pay the tariff."

"I know, I know." Maximilien waved Jehan away. He then lifted the latch and opened the gate.

The usual members came in, noses in the air and paying little attention to the monks. Jehan watched them make their way to the chapel, each holding whatever they were going to donate for the day.

Then, he noticed something odd. Only four people who were not official members paid the tariff and entered. The back of the chapel seated five times that many. Most days people were turned away because there wasn't room. Jehan stepped out of the gate and looked down the road. There wasn't anyone else in sight.

Abbot Ignace wasn't going to like this. No, he wasn't going to like this one bit.

❧

Ignace enjoyed being thought of as a man of vision. Not only from the visions he received from the Lord, but also his vision of the future. It was a future where his name would be spoken along the likes of Moses, Noah and Jesus. Yes, Ignace found that vision of the future very appealing, and it would come true—if people did what they were told.

During the last few services, fewer people were

paying the tariff to watch, though he didn't know why.

As he thought about it, he received another vision. He needed people to realize the importance of attending, and the consequences of failing to do so.

He stood at the altar mid and counted only four non-members—the true believers were all in attendance, as they should be.

"We've been offered a great gift from the Lord in the diamond divine," Ignace started. He noticed people nodding their heads in agreement. "However, there are those that still don't believe and aren't willing to make the needed sacrifices to receive its blessings. To that end, the Lord has given me another vision."

He paused for a moment, making sure all eyes were on him. "This vision left me blinded by the light, and it started right in front of my eyes. And I saw a burning chariot, and the four horsemen of the apocalypse waiting on high!"

Several people were shaking nervously in their seats at the image. Ignace continued, his voice booming throughout the chapel. "And I saw this land, a battlefield, with a hundred thousand men fighting hand to hand."

The war was still fresh enough on their minds that he knew the fear this statement would bring. "However, because of the faithfulness of this people, something wondrous happened. I heard the sounds of victory and the rivers ran red with the blood of our enemies!

"And I saw fire from the sky! I saw fire, and I saw paradise! Fire from the sun, I saw fire and I saw alpha and omega—the beginning and the end! Those who were true believers were saved. And those who weren't? They were left in the night, trembling in fear. Which side will you be on?"

Ignace didn't let any respond to the rhetorical question. "I have seen to the future, and the future is here! Through the diamond divine we will be saved. Who will be the first blessed today?"

All the members of his congregation stood at once, begging to go first. Those in the back, the non-members, slipped out of the chapel doors.

Good, Ignace thought, *they will go tell those who are not attending the error of their ways.*

ᨖ

"I'm never going back to the chapel," the drunken man next to Gaubert said in a slurred voice. "My money's better spent here, listenin' to Christophe. Now he's one that understands the common man, what with losing his wife and all. Yes, much better to be here."

This was not the first time Constable Gaubert had heard someone say they would rather spend their coin at the taverns then watch the abbot bless people. In fact, Christophe was now performing five nights a week, with tickets being sold in advance to avoid overcrowding. There had been the occasional fight that, as constable, he had to break up—usually because someone was turned away because there was no more room.

Gaubert made it a point to be here as often as he could. It wasn't only to keep the peace—he actually enjoyed the performances. Tonight, however, there was someone new that had come to watch.

The person had arrived early and remained hooded as they came in from the rain. They then went to the shadows of the upper level, even though there were plenty of good seats available on the main floor.

Christophe was his usual charming self, and Gaubert noted how many people were singing along with him—not only the well-known folk songs he sang, but also the songs that Christophe had written himself. From Gaubert's point of view, the singer could portray a lot of emotion in his songs, no doubt drawing from the passing of his wife and the other events of his life. It became obvious that his song *The Tower* was quickly becoming a favorite—and why not? It was hauntingly beautiful, plus it was something the common man could appreciate—riches could only buy so much in this life.

As the evening drew to a close, Gaubert watched the hooded man leave the tavern. Using the skills he learned as a scout during the war, the constable followed him into the night. He kept just far enough behind as to not rouse suspicion, but close enough to see where the man went.

After winding and doubling back down several streets, the hooded man drew close to the side of the Abbé. Then just like that, Gaubert lost him. The man had been close to the side of the Monastery, but then appeared to disappear into the wall.

Gaubert made note of where this happened and then slipped back into the night, fully intending to return when it was light enough to see where the man's tracks led.

ᴄᴙᴐ

Ignace couldn't believe what Florent was telling him. It didn't make sense. "You say a common street performer is the reason we've not had more people coming to watch the blessings?"

The wiry monk nodded. "I overheard several people say they would rather spend their money listening to him sing than to watch blessings bestowed on the faithful."

The abbot started to pace back and forth in his chambers. So, he was to be tested. And no wonder—he'd been successful in doing the Lord's will, now it seemed he'd caught the attention of the enemy of all mankind.

"Brother Florent," Ignace said. "Tell me about the songs this man is singing."

"They are mostly folk songs I heard growing up, though there are several he has claimed to have written himself."

Ignace stopped pacing and faced the monk. "What kind of songs does he write?"

"Well, there was one I remember quite well," Florent said, scratching the side of his nose. "I don't remember the name of it, but it was about a rich man who hunted for pleasure. One day he found a woman in the forest, and he wanted her, and she agreed to go with him if he would stop hunting. He wouldn't, and he took her captive. It turns out she was a bird or something if I understood the song right. She flew away at the end."

"The woman in the song used magic to turn into a bird?" Ignace asked. He needed this point to be clear.

Florent frowned. "How else would she turn into a bird?"

"Blasphemy!" Ignace pronounced. "This singer is a heretic most foul. He's obviously been sent by the devil to corrupt our noble work here."

He poked Florent in the chest. "Tomorrow, you and Jehan will bring this man to me. I will not allow the devil to win!"

ɞɞ

The knocking on Christophe's door was unrelenting. It was fairly early in the morning and he was still waking up. The first thing that came to Christophe's mind was that Didier had returned, even though he was told not to do so. Word had it that La boutique de désirs had fallen on hard times, and that Didier wasn't able to donate enough to the Abbé to be considered a member. Regardless, there was nothing Didier could offer that would be enough for Christophe to return.

"I'll be right there!" Christophe called as he climbed out of bed. The knocking stopped for a moment, but soon continued while he was getting dressed, and if anything, it was more insistent than before.

Christophe opened the door and instead of finding Didier, there were two of the Abbé's monks. One was thin with eyes that seemed to shift back and forth nervously. The other was tall and well built. He wasn't sure why the monks were at his door. Perhaps something happened to his son…

"Brother Florent, Brother Jehan," Christophe said. "Has something happened to my son Lucien?"

The monks looked at each other, appearing confused by the question. "No, no, nothing like that," Brother Florent said. "Abbot Ignace told us to bring you to the Abbé."

This was very odd. Christophe had been saving every coin he could to buy eternal life for his family. It would take him quite a while to earn the amount needed, but at the rate he was making money at the tavern, it would happen. There was even talk of Jourdain arranging for him to go to other towns to sing his songs—word had spread of his performances and the tavern owner was convinced together they could make a good amount of money by doing so.

"Why does the abbot want to see me? I've been working very hard to earn enough to join the congregation, but as of now, I don't have the full amount of money I need," Christophe said.

Brother Jehan was about to say something when Florent interrupted him. "Just get whatever coin that you have saved. But be quick about it—the abbot doesn't like to be kept waiting."

Christophe hurried to the back room where he hid his savings. Perhaps the abbot had heard about his goal of saving up and was showing mercy. Perhaps Ignace would allow him to make the donation now, and at a reduced amount due to his hard work and faith. With hope swelling in his chest, Christophe set off with the monks to the Abbé St. Pierre.

ଓଃ

Gaubert tapped his foot impatiently as he waited. On two different occasions he had to threaten the monk at the monastery gate to let him in. Today, however, he was told he needed to come to the Abbé, and from Brother Bastien's tone of voice, it didn't sound like a request.

He didn't like how the abbot held power over him. Thus far, as long as Gaubert kept his distance and left these so called holy men to do their business unimpeded, he was left alone in turn.

It was interesting to Gaubert on what transpired when he arrived at the Abbé. There were some harsh words exchanged between Brothers Bastien and Maximilien. From what Gaubert could surmise, Maximilien was supposed to go with Bastien, but the other monk said it was too far to walk. Maximilien had gotten quite a bit heavier since the last time Gaubert visited the Abbé.

"Can you now tell me why I'm here?" Gaubert asked Bastien.

The monk shook his head. "The abbot will explain everything." And with those words, it was evident he had no more to say on the subject.

Moments passed in uncomfortable silence until the gate to the Abbé opened. Gaubert was surprised to see the singer, Christophe, being escorted by Brothers Florent and Jehan.

"Remain here," Florent said. "I'll fetch the abbot."

After the monk departed, Christophe said, "Good morning to you, Constable."

"To you as well, Christophe." He thought of asking why the singer was here, but decided it was best to wait.

It wasn't long before Abbot Ignace exited of the chapel and approached them, with Brother Florent trailing behind.

"You are Christophe, correct?" the abbot asked. "We buried your wife not long ago, right?"

"You're correct on both accounts, Abbot," Christophe said, bowing his head in reverence.

Ignace folded his arms. "Tell me, why haven't you dedicated yourself to the Lord?"

"I—uh—I mean to say," Christophe stuttered. "I've been working hard to earn enough to join the congregation." He held up a pouch that appeared to be filled with coin. "I'm saving enough to buy the promise of eternal life for me and my family."

The abbot held out his hand for the pouch, which Christophe gave eagerly. Ignace handed the money to Florent then frowned at the singer.

"But how have you been earning the money? Didn't you use to work for Didier?"

Gaubert had no idea why the abbot insisted he, the constable, was here to watch this conversation.

"I once worked for Didier, yes." Christophe appeared as confused as Gaubert was feeling. "But I've since been—"

He was cut off by Ignace. "You've since been spending your time in a tavern, surrounded by drunkards, and telling tales that mock the Lord."

"What? No, I—"

"Have you or have you not been singing songs that involve magic?" the abbot asked.

Christophe's eyebrows lowered as he thought on what he had been asked. "There are elements of fantasy in some of the songs, yes. But they are used to teach a message."

"Anything that is not done to glorify the Lord is against His will," Ignace said. He pointed a chubby finger at Christophe. "You've been luring people away from the Abbé with your insidious songs."

Gaubert now understood. He had come back the morning after he followed the cloaked person to the Abbé. Unfortunately, it had rained the night before so all tracks had been washed away. But by his size and the way he carried himself, Gaubert bet it was Brother Florent who had been to the tavern. Florent must have overheard the same conversations about how people would rather spend their money listening to the singer than to watch the abbot give blessings.

"No, Abbot." Christophe was shaking. "I meant no disrespect."

"None-the-less, you've been doing the devil's work. Your public meetings are a danger to the state of all that is right and good. And they must be stopped."

Before Christophe could say another word, Ignace turned to Gaubert. "This man must be jailed until which time the Lord feels he is truly repentant."

Gaubert fought the urge to argue. He understood that he was a puppet in all of this—doing the abbot's bidding under the guise of the law.

"But, Abbot," Christophe said, "what of my money? Please, please use it as a donation to bless my wife and child with the promise of eternal life!"

Ignace's eyes grew large. "You are not worthy to receive any blessings. Instead, we will take this and use it for the building of the new temple, hoping the Lord will consider this when you face him on judgment day."

The abbot pointed to the gate. "Now, away with you—both of you. And may you one day be free of the devil's grasp."

Chapter 15

"Lucien!" came a cry from outside Fabrice's shop. "Come out, Lucien!"

Fabrice looked up from the wooden plank he was sawing. "Well, Lucien, you better go see what's going on so we can get back to work."

His mentor had been very patient with him during his apprenticeship. At the same time, he was clear on what was expected—and today they needed to finish their current project, a large wardrobe made of cedar.

"I won't be but a moment," Lucien said. He got up from his workbench and stepped out into the sunlight.

Henri and Guy were standing there, both looking distraught. "What's the matter?" Lucien asked upon seeing them. "Did Guy's father get accused of something else?"

"Not my father." Guy shook his head back and forth furiously. "Yours!"

His friends had played jokes on him before, so he didn't give this latest announcement much weight. Lucien looked up at the sky. The sun had yet to reach its highest point. "My father's probably not even awake yet. How could he be in trouble?"

"Word has spread that people saw him being taken to prison. They say he has been accused of heresy!" Henri said.

"Heresy?" Lucien asked. Now he knew they were trying to trick him. "Of all the people in town, why would anyone accuse him of heresy? And who are these 'they' people you heard this from?"

Henri took Lucien by the elbow and pulled him close. "Merchants, peddlers, people on the street. People that I know and have no reason not to trust when it comes to this," he whispered. Lucien knew that Henri had connections, and not necessarily the kind someone of his status should have. For the first time since he'd been called out from the shop, Lucien actually believed there was something wrong. Both Henri and Guy seemed very sincere.

"Let me go talk to Fabrice and tell him what happened," Lucien said, already beginning to remove his work gloves. "He'll let me go to the prison and see what this is all about."

❧

Gaubert shook his head. "I'm sorry, but he's not allowed to leave the prison."

"I'm not asking you to let him out," Lucien said, his voice cracking. "I'm just requesting to talk to him."

The constable was a muscular man, with scars along his arms which Lucien guessed to be from his battles in the war. From what he had heard, Gaubert didn't believe in the new religion Ignace had formed. Why he had agreed to keep his father prisoner on the charges of heresy seemed out of character. However, it seemed many people had changed since the diamond had arrived.

Gaubert stood with his arms folded. He gazed

down at Lucien and appeared to be debating the matter in his head. Finally, his features softened. "All right, you can speak with him. But be quick."

"Thank you, Constable," Lucien said. He then turned to Guy and Henri. "And thank you, my friends, for coming to get me."

Henri tilted his head. "That's what friends do, Lucien. We help each other out."

"Aye, now go see to your father," Guy said.

The constable stepped aside enough for Lucien to enter. The prison was mostly underground—almost a mini dungeon in some ways. Barred windows were along the top of the prison cells. There were six of the small rooms in all, three on each side. Lucien walked down the stone steps slowly, trying to think of what he'd say to his father. Heresy? It didn't make sense. His father had done everything he could to join Ignace's new religion.

All the doors were opened aside from the one on the far end to the left. Upon arriving, Lucien knocked on the solid wooden door, noting the latch had a large metal lock on it.

"What do you want, Constable?" came his father's tired voice behind the door.

"It's me, Father."

"Lucien! What are you doing here?"

"I could be asking you the same question."

His father chuckled, though there was no mirth in it. "Oh, Lucien, Lucien…" There was a drawn out pause, and then sounds of his father sobbing.

"Father, what is this talk of heresy? Surely you are innocent."

"My songs, my stories," came the muffled reply. "I meant no harm. They were just stories, in no way meant to be sacrilegious."

Lucien leaned closer to the door. "You're imprisoned because of your songs? I don't understand."

"The abbot said that because magic was in my songs, I was doing the devil's work."

It took a moment for Lucien to understand what his father was saying. At first, he interpreted the comment to mean the way his songs made others feel—it was almost magical. But that wouldn't have been enough to accuse him of heresy, would it? And then Lucien understood. It was the songs that had fantastical aspects, like *The Tower*. How was this against the Lord? They were just stories that taught a message in a way that stirred people's imaginations.

"This isn't right," Lucien said. "Can't the constable or the other monks see that?"

There was no reply from the other side, which of course, was his answer. Lucien tried something else. "Please, tell me how I can help."

"There's only one thing that can absolve me of my sins—the diamond divine. I was close, Lucien, to being able to save your mother. So close…"

His father started crying again. It was a sound so profoundly sad that Lucien fell to his knees. It would take years for Lucien to earn enough money to pay for a redemption, but still, if that was the only way his father felt he could be forgiven, he'd do it. "I'll help you, Father. I promise you, I will. But you must stay strong."

"I don't know if I can, son. Inside, I feel so… cold. I lost your mother, and now I've lost you."

"You haven't lost me, Father. I'm here," Lucien

said, trying to be brave. "Until I can help you, carry me like a fire in your heart. Will you do that?"

The crying from inside the cell subsided. "Yes, son. Thank you."

"I'll come back as soon as I can."

Lucien brushed the moisture from his eyes and took in several deep breaths before he left the prison. Henri and Guy would most likely be waiting outside for him, wanting to know what happened. He wasn't sure what to tell them that they hadn't already heard. The constable was still standing at the entrance.

"Thank you for letting me see him, Constable," Lucien said.

Again, to Lucien, the man seemed to be struggling with something inside himself. "It's not quite that easy," the constable said. He placed a hand on Lucien's shoulder. He had a firm grip, but not enough to cause pain.

"I don't understand. What's not so simple?"

"The abbot has declared your house as church property due to the nature of your father's crime."

"What?" Henri asked. He pointed to his friend. "That house belongs to Lucien now and he's done nothing wrong!"

The constable ignored Henri's comment. He instead had his full attention on Lucien. "The abbot said the house was church property. He didn't say anything about the contents inside the house. If I were you, I'd get there as soon as I could and take whatever I felt is of value."

"But where am I going to live?" Lucien asked, still stunned by the constable's announcement.

"With me," Henri said. "He's going to live with

me." When Henri used that tone of voice, there was no arguing with him.

The constable looked up to the sky. "I'd say I won't be able to secure your house until dark—I have other duties to attend to. It would be best if anything you needed was removed by then."

Lucien understood that somehow the constable was being coerced by the abbot, though he didn't dare ask how or why. He just knew that the man had given him a gift—one he wouldn't squander.

"Understood," Lucien said. It was hard to keep his emotions under control, but he needed to think clearly now. He then addressed Henri and Guy. "Thank you, Henri. You are most generous. And also, thanks to you, Guy."

Guy looked confused. "What did I do?"

"Aside from being a good friend, surely you will help me move what I can to Henri's."

"Uh, yes," Guy said. Henri and Lucien shared a knowing smile. Guy did whatever he could to avoid any kind of work—especially the kind that made him sweat.

"I need to go tell Fabrice what is going on, and then I'll meet you at my—I mean, what once was my house."

ꕥ

Henri's house was big. It was so large, in fact, that it had a spare room Lucien could use. It was upstairs, near the roof, but it seemed dry. Lucien couldn't imagine having a spare room in a house.

When they went to get the items Lucien thought were valuable, he took his father's lute, some crafts his mother had made, and the few trinkets Lucien had gathered over the years.

They left any furniture and household items behind, primarily for two reasons. First, Lucien had reasoned that if one of the abbot's monks noticed there was too much missing, it might cause problems for the constable. Second, he really had no place to store them. The room Henri provided was of a decent size—it was bigger than what he had before—but it wouldn't have enough space to store all his family's possessions.

It wasn't until that night, when Lucien was alone, that he really confronted his feelings. His mother had died recently, and the pain from her loss was still fresh. While his father was still alive, it was as if he had been taken away as well.

He lay on his bed, knees tucked to his chest, and cried. Throughout the war, they had lived in constant fear, but now that it had ended, there seemed to be hope. To have that taken away from him so soon seemed like a cruel act. Why would God do this to him? What had he done to upset Him?

Lucien pondered on that for a moment. No. It wasn't God. It was the abbot and his men. It was because of them that his father had had to work so much. Oh, not directly—but because Didier wanted more and more money to donate to the abbot. His father became so entranced by the idea of the diamond's ability to grant blessings and redemptions that he missed out on what was going on around him.

It wasn't until his mother died that his father realized what he had been missing. Things started to look better after that. Though his father was still hurting from his mother's death, he had found new happiness and purpose in his storytelling and singing. But once again, the abbot had taken that away.

A light knocking on the door brought Lucien out of his thoughts. He dried his cheeks and then sat up. "Come in."

The door opened just enough for Henri to poke his head in. "I came to check on you."

"I'm doing fine," Lucien said. He reached up and made sure he hadn't missed any tears.

Henri opened the door enough to step inside. "Well, you're a stronger person than I would be in the same situation. When my father died in the war, well, I didn't sleep much for weeks. I didn't want to be home—too many things reminded me of him."

"I guess that would explain why you prefer to spend as much time away from home as possible."

His friend's forehead creased. "Come to think of it, that does make sense." Henri closed the door behind him. "So, what are we going to do?"

"We?" Lucien asked. "What do you mean by we?"

Henri folded his arms. "While I want very much to become a member of Abbot Ignace's congregation, primarily to get to know the important people in the region, I don't agree with what he did to your father."

"Obviously, I don't either," Lucien said. He shrugged. "But what can we do? We can't break my father out of prison. He'd be a wanted man."

Henri came over and sat next to Lucien. "How do you think your father is feeling right now?"

“If he’s feeling anything like I am, he’s miserable.”

“And what can we do to lift his spirits?”

Lucien chewed on his lower lip as he thought. “I don’t know. He seemed so set on getting a blessing from the diamond divine.

“However, I doubt the abbot would let him get close to the famous gem now.”

Henri leaned in closer and whispered, “But what if we brought the diamond *to* him?”

“You mean … steal it?” Lucien asked, shocked.

“No, no. Not steal. Borrow. We’d just borrow it at night, then take it to the prison and let your father touch it through the barred window of the prison. After he touched it, we could convince him his sins were absolved, and then we could return it without anyone knowing it was gone.”

Lucien looked at his friend doubtfully. “There are so many problems with that plan, I’m not sure where to begin.”

“Like what?” Henri looked offended. “Before you say anything else, let me tell you that I’ve put a lot of thought into borrowing the diamond for myself. I’ve figured out a plan. This situation just gives us a good reason to do it.”

“For starters, what makes you believe my father will agree to this? What would we tell him about how we got it?” Lucien asked.

“I’ll tell him I made a large donation to bring the diamond to him. I’ll tell him the abbot agreed only because he couldn’t have your father in the chapel after declaring him a heretic.

“We’ll tell him that all he needs to do is touch the diamond and he will be forgiven.”

Lucien rolled his eyes. This plan was becoming more and more difficult to believe. While he thought that Henri honestly wanted to help, he suspected that his friend's motives were more selfish in getting a chance to handle the diamond himself. "And why would you make such a donation for my father?"

"Why for the good of the people, of course," Henri said. "The townsfolk enjoy his performances. Once he has touched the stone, I'll tell him to confess to the abbot his sins and that he will do everything he can to help promote the church from that point forward. Of course, he'd have to sing only songs approved by the church, but I'm sure he'd be willing to do that."

"And when word spreads that you helped free my father, as I'm sure it will if you have any say in the matter, you will become a hero of sorts, right?"

Henri smiled. "It would be a positive side effect, yes."

For the first time, Lucien started to feel hope. That was, until, he remembered something unpleasant. "But what about the stories of people who tried to steal the diamond and ended up headless in the river? And how would we even get in and out unnoticed?"

"We aren't *stealing* the diamond, we are *borrowing* it," Henri emphasized once again. "There's a big difference. As for getting in, I've discovered a secret way on the side of the Abbé the monks use time and again." He patted Lucien on the shoulder. "We can do this."

"I don't know—" Lucien began to say.

Henri interrupted him. "You don't have to

decide now. There is a new moon in a couple of days—a perfect time to go because it will be very dark outside. Just promise me you'll think on it."

After hesitating for a moment, Lucien nodded. "All right, I'll think it over."

ଔଓ

"I love the night," Henri declared. He then took in a deep breath. "It's like I can be someone else—a complete transformation from the person I am during the day."

"Oh, I don't know," Guy said. "You don't seem much different to me than during the daytime."

Henri harrumphed. "Now that I'm getting older, I need to be seen as more respectable. But during the night…now, that's when I can be whoever I want."

The statement unsettled Lucien. Henri was an overall good person, though he walked the line between right and wrong pretty closely. Lucien referred to Henri as "the man on the line" on more than one occasion—his friend didn't find it amusing.

Henri, Guy and Lucien were all dressed in dark clothing. It was to help them hide in the shadows easier, or so Henri had told them. Lucien had struggled with deciding to go along with his friend's plan. However, Henri kept reassuring him that everything would be fine and had finally swayed him. Guy had been easy to convince. As long as Henri said to do it, Guy did it.

Music from the taverns sounded in the

distance, even though it was almost closing time. There was an occasional person walking the street, but so far they had been able to avoid anyone.

"Are you sure we shouldn't wait a bit longer?" Lucien asked.

"Nah, this is the perfect time. It's late at night, but not so late that if we get spotted it would be suspicious. Sure, there are a few people about, but don't worry, we'll take the back ways."

Lucien couldn't fault his friend's logic. "Fine. But are you sure you can find your way in the dark?"

"Oh, yes." Henri tapped the side of his head. "I'm reading from a map in the mind."

Without saying anything else, Henri started sneaking toward the Abbé.

ଓଓ

Gaubert sat on a stool outside the prison. The night was a bit on the cooler side, but he had a drink to keep him warm. The last two nights he had gone to the tavern as normal, however the entertainment on display didn't interest him. One of the singers was somewhat talented, but not compared to Christophe. It was a crime that Christophe had been imprisoned. Gaubert paused at that thought and then laughed at the irony of it all.

ଓଓ

"It's just through there," Henri pointed to some bushes, as tall as a man, along the side of the Monastery's wall.

Lucien squinted. "Are you sure? It looks just like more wall."

His friend smacked him lightly on the shoulder. "I've seen monks come and go from this spot. There is an opening there. Go! See for yourself."

Lucien looked around and didn't see anyone about. Then carefully, he stepped out from the shadows and quickly went to the bushes. It was hard to see in the dark, but on either side of the evergreens there was nothing but a solid wall.

He took a step back and inspected the bushes themselves. There were two big ones, with thick branches that overlapped each other. These were not unlike many of the others that surrounded the Abbé, so Lucien wondered if Henri had remembered the right spot.

He had an idea and stuck his arm in-between the bushes. He leaned in far enough until his hand touched the wall beyond. Surely Henri had to be mistaken. He tried to push against the wall, but it didn't budge. He tried again, with a little more force and in the process, lost his balance, falling head first toward the wall.

Lucien thought for sure he would have hit his head, but hadn't. He was on all fours with most of his body between the bushes. He couldn't see a thing, so he felt out with his hand. After a moment, he touched something cold and hard—the wall, but it was going the wrong direction. Instead of being in front of him, it was beside him. Lucien reached up and felt stone above his head.

And then he understood. The entrance was about waist high off the ground. He started crawling forward with one hand sweeping back in forth in front of him. It wasn't long until he felt the needles of evergreen bushes in front of him. Pressing forward, he crawled until he was on the other side.

Lucien stood and looked around. Even though he could barely see, he could tell he was inside the Abbé's walls.

ଓଃ

Jehan lay next to Ambre in their usual spot by the garden. Soon, it would be too cold to be outside at night. In the meantime, Ambre met him here as often as they could. Even though she was convinced they were pre-forgiven and therefore doing nothing wrong, Jehan couldn't shake the feeling that deep inside, he knew better.

Still, he enjoyed hearing her breathe softly by his side. And she made him feel like he never thought possible. Which was more important? Enjoying life or listening to that inner voice of what was right and wrong? He pondered that as he stared into the night sky.

ଓଃ

Lucien crept forward, looking this way and that to make sure no one was around. The chapel was ahead and to the left, and through the windows along the top of the chapel walls, he could see the flickering of candlelight. Surely it was late enough that no one was still in the chapel.

A noise from behind him made him spin around in fright. He went to flee until he realized it was just Henri coming through the bushes with Guy right behind him.

"Over here," he whispered.

Henri and Guy snuck up beside him. Lucien pointed to the chapel. "There are candles still burning in the chapel. What do we do now?"

"There are always candles lit in the chapel," Henri said. "Didn't you know?"

"But why?"

Henri made a frustrated sound. "I don't know, I've just been told as such. Now, come on! Let's move before we're discovered."

The three teenage boys made toward the chapel, stopping now and again to make sure the way was clear. Once they reached the chapel door, Henri motioned for Lucien to open it. Even though Henri claimed that they were in no danger because they were only borrowing the diamond, Lucien noticed his friend was reluctant to do anything first.

Slowly, Lucien opened the chapel door and peeked inside. Along the walls were several candles, each flickering. Up on the altar high was the diamond divine, resting on a purple velvet pillow.

He opened the door a bit further and cringed when it made a creaking noise. He waited a moment. The sound didn't seem to alert anyone. Then carefully, he slipped inside, with Henri and Guy following.

"Hurry," Henri whispered urgently. "You're this close. Show me you have the guts to go up there and touch it."

Lucien didn't like to be dared into doing things. But he had come this far. For a moment, an image of something supernatural cutting off his head when he touched the diamond appeared in his mind. He was frightened, of that there was no doubt. At the same time, he wasn't doing this for himself. He was doing this out of the love he had for his father. If taking the diamond to his father would bring peace to his tortured soul, it was worth the risk.

He cautiously walked to the altar high and then climbed the stairs that would allow him to reach the diamond divine.

As close as he was, he noticed the diamond was the most beautiful thing he had ever seen. It was a gem, yes, but also something more. It was something he felt inside, and couldn't put into words. Surely such a wondrous item had to be a gift from God.

With an inner warmth and peace he'd felt on only the rarest of occasions, Lucien reached out and touched the diamond. And when he did, the whole place exploded with a great and wonderful light.

Chapter 16

Gaubert fell off his stool when something appeared in the direction of the Abbé St. Pierre. He had nearly dozed off when a light lit up the night sky. At first he thought it must be lightening, but there were no storm clouds—and the light remained constant. Secondly he thought there must be a fire blazing, yet there was no smoke and it didn't flicker.

The only other thing that came to mind was the diamond divine. But the abbot never gave blessings at night, and even when Gaubert saw the diamond shine, it wouldn't have been bright enough to shine like it was now. And, there was something more. The light itself was different somehow. When he looked at it, he felt a calm, peaceful feeling—though it didn't make sense.

He noticed that other people who were still awake had seen the light as well, and they started to head toward it.

He needed to investigate what was happening at the Abbé—and quickly.

ଔଓ

Ambre shook Jehan awake. The monk slowly opened his eyes. It couldn't be morning already, could it? There was light in the sky, though it didn't seem to be the morning rays.

As he awoke further, he realized that the light wasn't coming from the east, where the sun rose. No, it was coming from the north—where the Abbé stood.

"What's that glowing, Jehan?" Ambre asked.

He propped himself up on one elbow. He had seen something like this once before. It was the night that the old man, Geoffrey was his name, brought the diamond divine to the Abbé. When Geoffrey handled the gem, it emitted a glow so profound it made Jehan want to cry in joy. It was something that the abbot and the monks had failed to reproduce. And yet, here it was again.

Jehan reached for his robe. "I need to get to the Abbé—now."

"I don't understand," Ambre said. "What is it? What's causing that light?"

"The diamond divine," he said. He pulled the robe over his head. If he and Ambre were seeing this, so was everyone else in town.

Ambre reached for her clothing. "At night? And I don't remember seeing it shine like that."

"I must go," was all Jehan said in response.

"And I'm going with you," Ambre stated.

Lucien stood, his eyes transfixed on the diamond. While the light was strong, it didn't hurt his eyes. It was more than pure white—there were elements of blue, red and green. And accompanying the illumination was a feeling of peace and happiness. It reminded him of being held in his mother's arms, or the way he felt when his father praised him for something he had done.

He heard Henri and Guy gasp at first, but for a long drawn out moment after, they remained quiet. Finally, Henri seemed to realize that the light from the diamond was shining through the chapel's windows, no doubt alerting people to their presence.

"What did you do, Lucien?" Henri said. "Quick! Bring it here before we get caught."

Lucien looked down at his friend. Though he felt peaceful, his mind recognized the danger they were in. He picked up the diamond and carefully worked his way down the stairs from the altar high.

"Here, let me hold it," Henri said. He held out his hands.

Upon reaching his friend, Lucien gently gave him the diamond. The light still shone, though it dimmed considerably with different hues displayed.

"Let me touch it," Guy begged, after watching Henri hold it for a moment. "Please."

Henri seemed a bit reluctant to release the diamond, but then let Guy take it. Again the light changed, and to Lucien, it seemed to brighten slightly. Different colors were more pronounced when Guy held it compared to Lucien or Henri.

It was as if once Henri let go of the diamond that he came to his senses. "We need to go—now!"

Guy was enraptured by the gem while Lucien and Henri made their way to the chapel door. They opened it quickly, ignoring the loud creaking sound it made. They stepped out and closed the door behind them.

Henri pointed to the way they had entered. "We need to get beyond the wall. And we'll need a way to cover the diamond—to hide its glow."

"Why would we want to hide it?" Guy asked. His voice seemed distant. "It's the most beautiful thing I've ever seen."

"And it's the last thing you'll ever see if we get caught. Now hurry! Before we get spotted."

"'Tis too late for that," a voice said from across the Abbé's courtyard.

A monk stepped away from the front gates. He was thin and approached them with the calculated movements of a snake. "You boys should know what happens to people who try to steal the diamond." He reached into his robe's sleeve and pulled out a wicked looking knife. "The only question now is which of you will go first."

Henri made an attempt to run to the wall, but the monk was quicker. It was obvious that Henri wouldn't make it in time.

Lucien found the whole situation quite surreal. Guy continued to hold the diamond and appeared to be completely entranced. Even though it wasn't shining as brightly as when Lucien held it, it was still bright enough to light the area quite well. The comforting emotions he felt from the diamond were in complete contrast to the threats coming from the monk.

"No, you won't be getting out that way," the monk said. He moved to the bushes that hid the passage. "And the gates are barred shut. There's no escape."

Henri held his hands up. "We weren't going to steal it. We were just borrowing it. We would have returned it."

"You honestly don't expect me to believe that,

do you?" the monk asked.

He pointed the knife at Guy. "Now, you, the chubby one. Put the diamond down."

"Do it!" Henri yelled to his friend.

Guy appeared to come to his senses enough to understand what was happening. He went to set the diamond down when the sound of the bushes rustling caught everyone's attention.

The monk with the knife turned quickly to face whatever was coming through. Emerging from the bushes was a large monk, with a rather striking woman following closely behind.

"Jehan! What are you doing here?"

The large man looked at his fellow monk. "We saw the light and came to see what happened. Why do you have your knife drawn, Brother Florent?"

Pointing to Lucien and his friends, Florent hissed, "These boys were trying to steal the diamond divine!"

Jehan took a step forward. "How did you—"

His question remained unasked as the sound of banging on the front gate interrupted him. Shouts of "Let us in!" came from the other side of the gate.

"Put it down!" Florent demanded. He took a step toward Guy.

Guy knelt and put the diamond on the ground. As soon as he let go of it, the light dimmed out quickly, leaving them all in the dark.

Cries of surprise came from the gate. It seemed a large amount of people had gathered and were now making quite the racket—demanding venomously to be let in.

"I can't see a thing!" Florent screamed. "Jehan, don't let them escape!"

The pounding on the front gate was replaced with the sound of people pushing against it, trying to get in. Lucien heard wood cracking and had no doubt that the townspeople would soon be within the Abbé's walls.

"Run!" Henri yelled.

"Where?" Guy answered. "I can't see my hand in front of my face!"

"Get the diamond!" Florent screamed.

꧁꧂

Ignace woke to the sound of people shouting. It usually took quite a bit to wake him from his slumber. He heard more loud voices, though he couldn't understand what they were saying.

With some effort, he got out of bed, stood, and put on his robe. His room was directly off the chapel—he was the only one blessed to have his quarters so close. He opened the door and stepped out into the chapel. Many candles were still burning, their flickering light making shadows dance on the walls. He turned his eyes to the altar high. The diamond was gone!

That had to be what the shouting was about. As quickly as his little legs would take him, he hurried to the chapel doors.

He opened them and stepped out into the courtyard. At almost that precise moment, the front gate of the Abbé gave way to the mass of townsfolk pushing against it. People spilt into the courtyard, several of them holding torches.

"Halt! All of you!" the abbot screamed. "How dare you defile this sacred place!"

For a moment, no one moved. Ignace scanned the courtyard. Aside from the people who had broken down the gate, he saw three boys, Brothers Florent and Jehan and Ambre, who was one of his church members. On the ground was the diamond divine. He wasn't sure what happened, but it appeared that the boys were trying to steal the famous gem and had been caught. But he didn't understand why the townspeople were here—or why they would break down the gate. One thing Ignace was sure about, the people had been riled up by something. And from the look in their eyes and the way they stood, they were dangerous.

ꕥ

Lucien could sense that something bad was about to happen. Though he wasn't sure why, the people from the town had been whipped into a frenzy. No doubt they had seen the light coming from the Abbé and were drawn toward it, like moths to a flame. After they had broken down the gate and entered the courtyard, their malice was focused on his friends. But when they first came to the gate, they hadn't been angry—something had changed. He did the only thing he could think of to calm the crowd.

He picked up the diamond divine.

Once again, light erupted from the gem and the sense of warmth and peace washed over Lucien. He saw several of the townsfolk stare at him in wonder. Those holding torches, almost brandishing them as weapons, lowered them. Even the abbot and his monks stood by and watched.

Lucien walked over to the crowd. Fabrice stood near the front. Lucien went to his mentor and held out the diamond. "We meant no harm. We were taking this to my father so he could be forgiven of his sins. Instead, we discovered something. It is some-thing wonderful. Please, see for yourself that this is truly a gift from God."

The large woodcrafter took the diamond from Lucien. As before, the diamond dimmed a little and the colors it emitted changed somewhat. Fabrice then handed it to the person next to him. From townsperson to townsperson the diamond was passed. For each person, there was a different effect, though one thing was constant. Everyone could make it shine.

Lucien watched as the constable took the diamond into his hands. He thought he saw tears come to his eyes.

☙❧

"No! Stop!" the abbot cried out. "Brother Florent, get the diamond from them!"

Florent quickly crossed the courtyard. A woman, of middle age and still wearing her nightcap, was holding the diamond now. For her, the color blue was most prominent. Before anyone could react, Florent was to her. Roughly, he pulled the diamond away.

Immediately the diamond went dark. Not even the slightest hint of light shone from it. The townspeople noticed this and started talking amongst themselves. In the light from the torches, Ignace watched as Florent backed away. The monk spun and raced toward the chapel.

When he reached the abbot, Florent shoved the diamond at the church's leader. Startled, Ignace took the diamond. As with Brother Florent, no light.

Ignace had to do something to get control over the crowd. An idea popped into his head.

"I've turned off the diamond divine as a sign that you are not worthy of its blessings!" the abbot declared.

The crowd appeared to be in shock. *Good.* He needed to keep control over them. "And because of your lack of faith and disrespect you've shown on holy ground, the price of the donations will be doubled from henceforward! Now, return to your homes!"

For a reason Ignace couldn't understand, the people didn't move. The woman who held it last, spoke up. "Abbot, I don't understand. When I saw the light in the night sky, it was accompanied by a feeling I've not felt when attending your blessings. When I held it, the feeling was even stronger, and… oh, I'm not sure how to explain it, more personal."

Ignace didn't like that he was being challenged. "You've no doubt been drinking and your thoughts aren't clear. Now leave, before the donation prices go even higher!"

This time, another person spoke up. He was a man of great wealth and one of the congregation's most prominent members. "I've not been drinking tonight, and I experienced what she did just now. Abbot, I will give you your asking price for a blessing of pre-forgiveness for the upcoming week if you perform the blessing right now."

Ignace felt sweat trickle down the back of his

neck. "No! I will not do it! Your actions of breaking down the gates of the Abbé are proof you are not worthy."

"You *will* not? Or is it that you *cannot*?" the man retorted.

"I..." the abbot started to say; but then words left him. His heart sank. Undoubtedly the people noticed that when it came to the residents of the Abbé, one thing was clear: they could not make it shine.

"We've been tricked!" yelled a man. Ignace looked for the person who yelled that and recognized it was Didier. "I've given you all my possessions for what? I want them back! All of them!"

By now, hundreds of people were at the gate. Others started yelling as well, making demands of restitution. It was as if a dam broke and the people were the water.

"Florent! Jehan! Protect me!" Ignace screamed.

The two brothers raced to the abbot's side. Florent was still holding his knife while Jehan was so large and strong, most men would think twice before attacking him. The crowd began to approach them until someone called, "I think our gold and other donations are over here!"

A few men lingered and seemed to consider their odds against Florent and Jehan, but then they too went with the crowd.

At first, the constable tried to stop them, but he was no match for the angry mob. Instead, he turned his attention toward the abbot.

"Ignace! Bring the diamond here!" the constable called, still standing at the gate.

"I found the treasury!" a voice called from the far side of the Abbé. The crowd swept that direction.

From the crowd emerged Brothers Maximilien and Bastien, though both looked like they had been roughed up. Bastien's night robe was spotted with blood that appeared to be coming from his nose. The boys had sided up next to the constable, avoiding the mob as it ransacked the Abbé.

"Brothers," Ignace said, "We need protection. Follow me!"

They nodded in agreement and hurried to the constable. Ignace was still holding the darkened diamond.

"Constable Gaubert," the abbot said. "I demand your protection. The devil has gotten into the hearts of these people. Look at Brother Bastien for proof. They've drawn the blood of a holy man of the Lord!"

"The devil, you say? As in the master of all lies?" Gaubert responded.

The abbot's facial features twisted. "I know what you are implying, and I don't care for it."

The constable folded his muscular arms and stared at Ignace. "*I* don't care that you don't care. As I see it, these people have every right to be upset. And I'm pretty sure you will lose any influence you had with powerful men in the area."

Gaubert was right. Not only had he lost control of the people, he lost his leverage over the constable. But even still, he had to reason with the man.

Ignace took a step forward and whispered, "Don't you see? They'll kill me! As a man of the law, you are required to protect me."

The mob started to come out of the different buildings housed in the Abbé. Almost everyone had arms full of items, and pockets stuffed with coins.

There was some pushing and shoving as well as arguments over certain items. Some of the townspeople were clumped together, speaking to each other and pointing toward the abbot and his men. Ignace did not like the way they looked at him.

The constable spoke. "What is one of your favorite sayings, Abbot? 'The Lord helps those who help themselves?' I think it's about time you heeded your own advice."

"Meaning?"

The constable pointed to the crowd. "They want revenge. I've seen that look during the war when townspeople got a hold of an enemy soldier. Your only hope is to calm them down."

Several of the larger men in the crowd, each holding torches, started approaching the front gates where they stood.

"What can I do?" the abbot asked. He clutched the diamond divine as if it was his child.

"Give the diamond to Lucien, this boy here. He made it shine like no others," the constable instructed. "And then beg for forgiveness from this crowd—otherwise, there is nothing I can do that will stop them from taking your lives."

He couldn't give the diamond away. It was the key to everything! There had to be something else that could be done.

"Florent? Jehan?" the abbot asked of his two protectors.

"Too many of them," Florent said. He tossed

his knife aside and lifted his hands.

"Give the diamond to the boy," Jehan said. "It's the only way."

The mob kept advancing, and was gaining in numbers. Ignace felt like a trapped animal. He saw no other choice. In an act of desperation, he all but threw the diamond at Lucien. Once the boy held it, the diamond once again came to life, its wonderful glow illuminating the courtyard. Lucien's face reflected a sense of peace and joy.

It appeared the effect wasn't isolated to him. The men from the mob stopped, and many lowered their torches. Their expressions softened noticeably.

The abbot realized this was his moment. He fell to his knees and motioned for the monks to do the same.

Ignace cried out, "Eli, Eli, lama sabachthani? Please, I beg of you! Spare me!"

Next the monks began to speak. And in the end, many heard the brothers making confession of the things they had done. Bastien told how he had used the light of the sun to trick everyone. Florent told how he been instructed by the abbot to kill, all for the sake of the diamond. Maximilien simply blubbered, crying so hard his fat body shook with each sob. For the moment Jehan said nothing. The rest of the people had now gathered.

"Don't you see?" Ignace used his most penitent voice. "I've been tricked by the devil. I honestly thought I was doing the work of the Lord! I understand now that I am a victim, like all of you. Certainly, this must be clear! I beg of you, let me live so that I may repent!"

"But you killed people!" someone shouted.

Ignace held his hands up. "It wasn't me! It was Brother Florent. He did the killing. My hands were never bloodied."

Florent took exception to that statement. "Me? I was doing as you instructed!"

"You have your free will," Ignace countered. "If the devil didn't have power over you as well, you would have not gone through with the deeds."

Before anything else could be said, the constable interrupted them. "Good people of this town," he began, "I know you are angry and feel the need for revenge. But this is not the way. Killing them here and now will make your actions no more justified than what these men have done."

Gaubert turned his attention to the church men. "Ignace, and notice I do not use your title, you must leave this place and never return. Your crimes will be reported to the church and they will deal with you."

Though a few disagreed, most of the crowd murmured in agreement.

Brother Jehan realized it was over. His life of comfort. His life of easy work. Everything. What would he do next? Whatever it was, it wouldn't be with the church. But that would allow him to be with Ambre, wouldn't it? However, they would have to move away. He couldn't stay here.

And then there was the diamond. Seeing the boy hold it and make it shine reminded him of the first time he had seen it. He had forgotten how beautiful it was. They had taken something wondrous and perverted it.

Why would it shine for everyone else and not for the abbot or the monks? And then Jehan remembered what the old man, the one killed here at the these very gates, had called it. The abbot called it the diamond divine, and that was how it was known. But its name, its true name, was the mirror of the soul.

And seeing it shine now, Jehan understood why. "Before we go," he said, "there is something important I must tell you."

He pointed to the diamond and spoke before anyone could object. "When it was brought to us, the man who found it, the same man killed right here at these gates, called it the mirror of the soul. We had never referred to the diamond that way since. But I can see now why it has such a name. The boy holding it must have a kind soul. A worthy soul. The diamond, the mirror, reflects that. That's why it wouldn't shine for us. We were selfish. We were not worthy."

"That is Lucien," Fabrice said, stepping out in front of the crowd. "He's the son of Christophe, which many of you know from his performances. He's also my apprentice and I know him to be an exceptional lad. Your words ring true to me Jehan."

"Ignace," the constable said, "it is time for you and your men to leave."

The abbot nodded and got to his feet, with the monks rising right after.

Jehan looked toward Ambre who had stayed on the edge of the crowd. He wanted to call out to her, to have her rush to his arms. The expression on her face was unmistakable. It was one of disgust. Now, he knew, he had lost everything.

And the abbot led that sad procession as they went through the gate past the place where it had begun.

Chapter 17

"But what of the diamond?" Didier asked after the abbot and the monks left.

Gaubert eyed the merchant carefully. He knew this was a pivotal moment. "You mean the mirror of the soul, don't you Didier?"

"That was probably some nonsense the monk made up to save his own hide," Didier said. A few in the crowd echoed Didier's statement, but not many. "It's worth a lot of money."

"And what would you do if it was yours to sell?" Gaubert asked.

Didier puffed up his chest. "I have all sorts of connections. I am a well-known merchant, after all. I would take it to Paris and sell it to the highest bidder."

"After you got the money from selling it, then what?" Gaubert asked. The crowd seemed to hang on the merchant's response.

Motioning around him, Didier said, "Why, it would be given to the good people of the church who suffered so badly under Ignace's leadership. Of course, that would be minus the traveling costs and other fees for my time."

Gaubert watched the crowd's reaction. Some nodded at the idea, while others looked rather upset at Didier's recommendation.

"Listen, please, all of you!" the constable said,

addressing the crowd. "The long war is finally over. As a soldier, I can't even begin to tell you the horrors I witnessed. And do you know how it all began? I don't. But I do know this: simple disagreements often lead to much larger conflicts. Sometimes the dispute is over land rights, or over perceived insults, or even a woman." He placed a hand on Lucien's shoulder. "And sometimes, it's over objects of great worth. Are you willing to chance another war over something that should be treated with respect and reverence?"

The crowd seemed to take his words to heart. Didier started to argue his point, but was hushed by those around him.

"Then what is to become of the diamond?" someone from the crowd called out.

Gaubert considered the question for a moment. There was something about this diamond. Something he didn't understand. He held it himself, and it brought to him emotions he thought he'd never feel again. Yet, of all the people to handle the diamond, Lucien made it shine the brightest.

"Lucien, why are you here? How did the diamond come to your possession?"

The young boy licked his lips and then proceeded to tell them of his plan. Most in the crowd looked on in wonder at the selfless act Lucien described. Only when he finished did Didier speak up.

"You honestly expect us to believe you would have returned the diamond after your father had touched it?" the merchant asked.

Lucien looked stunned by the question. "Yes, I would have returned it."

"I believe he would," a voice from the crowd said.

Fabrice stepped forward. "I know he would have."

"Then, I suggest that the mirror of the soul is given to Lucien," Gaubert said. "With the promise that he'll keep it safe and that neither he nor his descendants will sell it for money."

Didier began to protest, but others shouted out their approval of the plan.

Gaubert faced Lucien. "Will you accept this responsibility?"

The boy nodded, seemingly in awe of what he'd been assigned.

"Now," the constable said, "let's go get your father, shall we?"

ઙ

Lucien walked down the street toward the prison, continuing to hold the mirror of the soul. The townspeople who had not already come out to see what was going on, watched from windows and door frames. A few people followed Lucien and Gaubert, including Guy, Henri and Fabrice. No one spoke, it seemed there was no need. The light and peace emitted by the mirror of the soul was enough.

They reached the prison, and Gaubert opened the front door, then walked down the stairs with Lucien following. The rest of those that had come had the respect to wait behind.

Gaubert knocked on the door where Christophe was held. Lucien couldn't wait to show his father. He knew the mirror of the soul would bring him peace, just not in the way his father had originally thought.

"What is it?" he heard his father ask from his prison cell.

The constable's response was to unlock the door and open it. His father sat curled up in a corner. He looked up and when he saw the mirror of the soul, he sat there, transfixed.

"Father," Lucien said. "I have brought this for you." He took several steps into the cell.

Christophe held out one of his hands toward the glowing gem. "How?" His voice cracked when he spoke.

"Please, just take it," Lucien said. He brought the mirror of the soul close enough that his father could reach it.

With hands shaking, Christophe took it from his son. The light changed colors somewhat, yet it remained as bright as when Lucien held it. The feeling emitted by the mirror of the soul also altered. While Lucien was still at peace, he felt something else. It was a feeling he struggled to identify—like everything was all right, a reassurance that there was no need for shame or guilt. And with that, Lucien understood what he was feeling.

It was forgiveness.

ঙ্গ

Lucien was almost done with his project. It had taken several days, and a lot of help from Fabrice, but before him was an ornate wooden box. It was of a fairly decent size, large enough to hold the mirror of the soul. A brass clasp in the front matched the hinges in the back. The box wasn't designed to be difficult to open—it wasn't meant to keep people out. Its purpose was to be a proper resting place for the gift he had been given.

"You've done a wonderful job," Fabrice said, admiring the box. "It's inspired work, if I've ever seen any."

Lucien felt himself blushing. "Thank you. I just had the ideas, it was your skill that made it come to be."

"Now don't sell yourself short, you did a fair amount of the work," his mentor said.

Rubbing a hand over the top of the smooth cover, Lucien said, "Do you think it worthy of the mirror of the soul?"

"It's certainly more fitting than where the monks had kept it."

"I suppose that's true."

Fabrice pointed to a flat place on the front of the box. "Have you decided what's going to be written here?"

"I've given it some thought, yes, but I've yet to make up my mind. When I do, I'll have it embossed in brass there, right below the clasp."

"Well, I'm sure you'll come up with something appropriate soon."

ↀ

The sun had set and dinner was done. Lucien was cleaning up—it was his turn—so Christophe sat by the window while he waited for his son to finish.

"Lucien, we need to leave," Christophe said.

"Leave? But we just finished dinner."

Christophe looked out into the autumn night. Three weeks had passed since he had been let out of prison. The constable made sure Christophe was given his house back, as well as the coin the abbot had taken. The money allowed him to rest and heal without having to worry about working.

"I don't mean tonight, son," Christophe said. "I mean we need to leave this area."

"You mean to move away?"

"Hear me out," Christophe said.

Lucien walked over and sat down next to him. "I'm listening."

"For the most part, people have respected the constable's mandate that they leave us alone, yet we still haven't felt safe enough to leave the mirror of the soul unattended. I fear it's just a matter of time before someone attempts to take it."

Lucien nodded. "Henri has mentioned the same thing. He's heard talk that Didier is still grumbling that he didn't get to sell it. But where would we go?"

"Your mother grew up north of here. It's where we were married. There is a beautiful church by a river. It's a lovely area."

His son didn't seem to take to the idea. "But, Father," Lucien said, "I thought you were going to return to performing again. I know people want to hear you—now more than ever. Will you be able to perform where we will move?"

"I'm sure I will," Christophe said. "People are always looking for good music and entertaining stories."

The horse Christophe bought was very strong and didn't seem to mind in the least to be pulling a cart. It was a good thing, too, because they had been traveling for several days, with a few more ahead of them. Christophe and Lucien had brought along a few of their more prized possessions, as well as food and clothing.

"I just wish you would have let me say good-bye to Henri and Guy," Lucien complained, not for the first time.

Christophe sighed. "Son, we've been over this. You said you understood why we had to leave without telling anyone where we were going."

Lucien looked back into the cart. He stared at the blanket that covered his finely crafted box—the box that contained the mirror of the soul. "I do. I understand that if people knew where we were headed, they might come after us to steal the mirror of the soul. But, I wouldn't have told my friends where we were going—just that we were leaving."

He felt his son's pain. Christophe had friends, yes, but that isn't who he would be missing. Rosette was buried by the Abbé. He had visited her grave often, and found some peace resting there.

"It was better that we didn't give anyone an idea that we were leaving, or when," Christophe said. "This way, hopefully they won't even notice we've been gone for several days."

"But what about Fabrice?" Lucien pointed out. "He would have known something was wrong when I didn't show up for work."

Christophe chuckled.

"What's so funny?" Lucien looked at his father intently.

"I told him you quit," Christophe replied.

Lucien appeared shocked. "What did you tell him was the reason?"

Christophe smiled at his son. "So you could become *my* apprentice."

ꟸ

A feeling of foreboding ran through Christophe as they approached the old church. The farms they had seen the last couple of days were deserted, many partially destroyed. There was evidence of heavy fighting in the area from the war—broken arrows, bits of armor here and there and even a decaying body now and again. Lucien was trying to act brave, but Christophe could tell the setting bothered him.

None of it looked to be recent activity, but it also meant that this would not be the place to settle down. However, he held onto some hope—perhaps there were people by the church.

Many years had fallen on that golden country morning when he and Rosette were married. Because of the war, they hadn't been back here since. He rounded a hill and saw the church—or at least what was left of it. It stood in ruins with its broken walls covered in ivy. Instead of turtledoves, there were ravens wheeling round above him.

"Is that it?" Lucien asked. His son looked shaken.

"It used to be."

He pulled the horse and cart up closer to the church.

"Stay here, son."

Christophe got down from the cart and made his way toward the last remaining headstone in an overgrown graveyard. He fell to his knees and read the line beneath the leaves that covered the grave marker.

Here lies fair Rosette
Loving mother and wife
Winter made her ill
And took her from this life

Tears filled his eyes. His wife, his Rosette, was named after her grandmother—which must have been the person buried here. Thinking of his dearly departed wife, he looked up the hill, where a rundown mill stood next to the river.

In his mind's eye, instead of the dreary late autumn evening, he saw an early spring morning. The graveyard was filled with growing flowers and once again, the turtledoves serenaded him from the belfry.

Walking toward him was Rosette in her wedding gown. Her smile matched the surrounding sunlight. In his head, he heard the song that was sung that day. About how he should let his love shine on.

He would do that. Even though his Rosette was gone, his love for her would shine on.

❧

For nearly a week they had traveled from the ruined church until they found a town of decent size. It had several taverns which seemed skeptical at first to allow Christophe to perform—that was until he offered to play for free one night.

He was an instant success.

In exchange for performing, he and Lucien were given a room to stay in and food to eat. He was teaching Lucien to play the lute, and so far, his son was doing very well.

It was early afternoon, and they just had their mid-day meal. Christophe strummed his lute while humming a tune. It wasn't any song in particular; just some notes he played that reflected his mood.

"That's pretty, Father," Lucien said. He was lying on his bed with his hands resting behind his head. "What is it called?"

Christophe tried to think of words that described the music, but nothing seemed fitting. "There isn't a name for it. Any suggestions?"

Lucien lay quietly for a moment. "I'm not sure. I was wrapped in my own thoughts when suddenly the sweetest music filled the air."

"Maybe I'll not add words then," Christophe said. "Maybe I'll just hum along."

Lucien nodded. "I think that would work. Maybe you can perform it tonight."

"Perhaps I will," Christophe said. "Or perhaps you can."

Lucien looked over at his father. "Oh, no. I'm not ready just yet. Though, I am getting more comfortable since we've been here."

"Yes, I like it here as well." Christophe returned to playing his song, experimenting with some different chord combinations.

After a few more moments, Lucien asked, "Father, do you think the mirror of the soul is safe here?"

"As safe as anywhere I suppose."

"But, shouldn't we share it with people? It seems too great of a gift to keep hidden."

Christophe stopped playing. "But what if it falls into the wrong hands again? Some people will see the mirror of the soul as something to sell or to use to influence people."

"Actually, that's something that's been bothering me," Lucien said. "Why did God allow the abbot to use the mirror of the soul to trick people?"

Though he had a few ideas on the subject, Christophe decided to see what his son would say. "Why do *you* think he would do that, Lucien?"

The teenage boy looked back up at the roof over his head while he thought. Soon, he answered, "There are a lot of things I don't understand—yet. Like when Fabrice was teaching me to become a woodworker, I had no idea how to begin. I learned little by little, and along the way, Fabrice would let me fail and make mistakes. I learned more from making mistakes than getting it right on the first try."

Christophe smiled. He liked hearing his son think things through.

"Just as when Fabrice would watch as I ruined something I was working on, perhaps God is doing the same."

Lucien continued. "Maybe He puts things before us, and lets us do what we will. Sometimes we make the right choices, sometimes the wrong ones."

"So you believe that the mirror of the soul is truly a gift from God?" Christophe asked.

Lucien didn't hesitate when he answered, "It has to be. Is it something I can explain? No. But there are a lot of things I can't explain. Why does a rainbow sometimes appear in the sky after a storm? Why is there a grave in the hills by the Abbé that is always covered in flowers? I think that God sends us things to help us learn, even if we don't understand it at the time."

"You make a good point," Christophe said, hoping Lucien would continue.

"After all," Lucien said, "the abbot pointed out that God gave Moses the tablets of stone with the ten commandments, and he also gave Noah the knowledge to build an ark. Who knows what else he'll reveal one day?"

Christophe hadn't thought of that, but it made sense.

"But back to the mirror of the soul," Lucien said. "What if someone was to take it and try to use it as the abbot did? Do you think God would let it happen again?"

"Perhaps the reason God let the abbot take it was not only to reveal the abbot for who he was, but also to teach the rest of us a lesson," Christophe said. "Consider the abbot and the monks. All their dreams of glory, all their schemes and stories would come to nothing after all."

"I don't understand," Lucien said. "The mirror of the soul isn't what the abbot claimed it to be. It can't give blessings or absolve sins. It reflects the soul of the one who holds it, both in feeling and light."

"I don't think it's as simple as that," Christophe said. "Do you remember how you felt when I held it in the prison cell?"

His son seemed to reflect for a moment. "I do, and I'm glad you asked. I've wondered about that. What I felt, for lack of a better explanation, was forgiveness."

"Exactly," Christophe said. "And if it doesn't offer blessings or forgiveness, then why were those feelings coming from me?"

"I don't know, Father," Lucien said. "But I can't deny what I felt."

Christophe rubbed his chin. "I've reflected back on that moment often since I was freed. You see, I believed that I had sinned in letting your mother die, and then being unable to earn the money needed to buy eternal life for all of us."

"Neither of those things were your fault."

"I know that now, but at the time I didn't. I believed that only the power of the diamond divine could grant me forgiveness. But that wasn't the case. I now realize I needed to forgive myself."

His son nodded, and then chewed on his lower lip. Christophe was happy his son was thinking about what he, himself, had realized.

"Also, could I have possibly extended your mother's life if I had given you the coin needed for the herbs or if I had come home? Perhaps. Or perhaps it was her time to go," Christophe said.

"Perhaps it was," Lucien said softly.

"As for your other question, will God let someone else use it? I don't know that for sure. But I felt very strongly that we needed to get away from the Abbé St. Pierre. Have you noticed neither of us has removed the mirror of the soul since we put it in the box you made?"

"I went to take it out once we got here, but I had a strong feeling I shouldn't."

Christophe nodded. "I've had that same feeling."

Lucien paused for a moment, still looking deep in thought. "But, Father, there is so much I still don't understand. Why did the diamond light for everyone but the monks? And why did it shine the brightest for me?"

This was something else Christophe had spent many days thinking about. He had come to only one conclusion. "It was your love for me that lit the mirror of the soul when you held it. It was my love for you and your mother that did the same for me. The power to make it shine doesn't come from man, or the abbot and his men would have been able to."

"Then where does the power come from?"

Christophe smiled at Lucien. "It comes from a power greater, from the world's creator. He gave us love to light the mirror of the soul."

Lucien considered that a moment. He then said, "I now know what to put on the front of the box."

Epilogue

Present day

"And what of that box, Cardinal Asaph?" Ira asked.

As a newly assigned priest to the cardinal, he was in awe of the powerful man. Asaph was well known for his collection of rare items he purchased in the name of the church.

"Brother Ira, you certainly are the curious one, aren't you? As my new assistant, I've honored your request to see my collection, which I have shown you. Please understand I've acquired these items over my lifetime, sometimes with little or no information about their origins. For that box, I know precious little."

"I almost didn't notice it back there in that dark, unlit corner," Ira said, slowly approaching it. "Tell me, please, what do you know about it?"

"All right, then after this we must return to our duties, are we clear?" Asaph asked.

"Yes, Cardinal, we're clear."

"Then proceed." Asaph motioned to where the item was stored.

Asaph spoke as he followed the priest to the box. "It's believed this container was made around the end of the Hundred Year's war, somewhere in the south of France.

"It was passed down through the bloodline of the person that made the box. During one of the many religious wars of the Seventeenth century, it disappeared. It was only recently found by some archeologists, who surmised its origin and history from tales of the locals in various areas. They placed it up for bid at an auction. I was drawn to the inscription on the front. It's embossed in brass, and somewhat faded, but it is still legible. Tell me, Ira, what does it say?"

The priest bent down and squinted in the dim light. "I believe it is in Latin."

"You would be correct," Asaph said. "Can you translate it?"

"I'll try." Ira mouthed the words and appeared to be deep in thought for several moments. He stood. "It says, 'Amor speculum anima lucet'. But I don't understand. I would translate it as 'Love lights the mirror of the soul.' But that seems like nonsense. What's in the box?"

Asaph shrugged. "I don't know."

"You've never opened it?" Ira was stunned. It didn't make any sense.

"Not only have *I* not opened it, neither has anyone else since it was found."

The priest frowned. "Why not?"

"It's hard to explain," the cardinal said. "I just don't feel, well, like I'm the one to open it. What's strange is that the archeologists and the people at the auction house had the same feeling. And they open everything. I tried several times, but on each attempt, I couldn't bring myself to do it. I had nearly forgotten about it until you pointed it out."

Ira looked at the box in wonder. "Surely you

are curious about its contents."

"Need I remind you of the stories of the curious cat, or Pandora's box?" Asaph asked.

The priest shook his head. "I know those stories, but they are just that—stories." He pointed to the box. "This is real."

"Then, by all means, open it." Asaph motioned to the box then took a step back.

Ira almost laughed at the idea that no one would open the box. But then stopped. Was this some sort of joke? Ira remembered seeing someone open what they thought was a can of nuts, only to have a fake snake spring out once the lid was off. Was this the same thing? It seemed out of character for the cardinal to pull such a prank. Well, he'd show the cardinal. He wouldn't jump or flinch when he opened the box.

Ira took a deep breath and steeled himself. He then reached out to undo the brass latch on the front of the box.

He felt something deep in his chest. It was something he'd not felt before. It was almost as if a hand was on his heart and lungs squeezing them. The closer his hand moved toward the box, the stronger the sensation became. It didn't hurt, per se, as much as it gave him the feeling he was about to do something he shouldn't. It was akin to stepping to the edge of a cliff and looking down, and trying to force your body to step over the edge. In the end, it was too powerful of an impression to ignore. He brought his hand away from the box, and in doing so, was able to relax his ridged body. He turned and faced Asaph.

"Cardinal, please forgive my pride and

boldness. I can't explain why, but I know I shouldn't open it."

Asaph placed his hand on Ira's shoulder. "My young priest, now you understand. The box will remain here until such a time as God sends the right person."

"The mirror of the soul…" Ira said, reverently. "Love lights the mirror of the soul. I shall ponder and pray about that."

"As well you should, my son, as well you should."

All through the world, there are many others
who always follow everything they are told
by men with rules and regulations,
using old superstitions and tales to assume control;

But all their dreams of glory,
all their schemes and stories,
will come to nothing after all.
Because a power greater
from the world's creator
gave us love to light the mirror of the soul;
Only love can light the mirror of the soul.

AMOR SPECULUM ANIMA LUCET.

LUCIFER EX INFERNO CLAMAT.

NE NOS INDUCAT IN TENTATIONEM.

AMOR SPECULUM ANIMA LUCET.

Love lights the mirror of the soul.

The devil is calling from hell.

Lead us not into temptation.

Love lights the mirror of the soul.

ABOUT THE AUTHOR

J. Lloyd Morgan is an award winning author and television director. He graduated from Brigham Young University with a degree in Communications and a minor in English. Morgan earned a Master's degree in Creative Writing in 2014.

He has lived all over the United States, but now resides in North Carolina with his wife and four daughters. Aside from writing, Morgan is an avid reader. He's also a huge fan of baseball and enjoys listening to music.

He is the author of the novels *The Hidden Sun*, *The Waxing Moon*, *The Zealous Star* and the forthcoming *Wall of Faith*.

His published short stories include *Howler King*, *I Heard the Bells on Christmas Day*, and award-winning *The Doughnut*.

An anthology of short stories, observations and insights called *The Night the Port-A-Potty Burned Down and Other Stories* was released at the end of 2012.

For more information, visit his website at www.jlloydmorgan.com

Made in the USA
Lexington, KY
04 April 2013